# CATSKILL MURDER MYSTERY

# Catskill Murder Mystery

## MINDY LITTMAN HOLLAND

Catskill Murder Mystery
Copyright © 2020 Mindy Littman Holland

Cover design by Mindy Littman Holland
Interior formatting by Grant Holland
Author photograph by Mindy Littman Holland

Visit the author's website at books.mindylittmanholland.com

Printed in the United States of America.

ISBN: 9798577173517

# DEDICATION

For Leo. I cared.

# CHAPTER 1

In the beginning, there were only four of us sharing a cabin: Susie Finnegan from Binghamton, New York; Clarice O'Hare from Dallas, Texas; Mary-Ann Dunn from Chatham, Massachusetts; and me, Amy Bernstein, from Manhasset, New York. It wasn't until later in the summer that Rita Connelly joined us, and we had no idea of where she was coming from. All we knew was that she wore a wig, was a grown woman in her thirties, and had a boyfriend named Rocco. The rest of us were still in our teens.

We were all a little afraid of Rita and a lot afraid of her boyfriend's name. But we kept our worries to ourselves because we had other things to concern ourselves with.

Susie of Binghamton was a sweet parochial school graduate and a natural blonde. She looked like a wholesome cheerleader. How she made her way into the Borscht Belt, I have no idea, but there was going to be plenty of trouble for her to get into in the Catskills.

Clarice of Dallas was also a parochial school graduate. She was very thin and wore her hair in a flip; a pretty girl who had premonitions of dying in a fiery car crash. She also seemed to have an eating disorder. It was going to be interesting to see how she handled capon and kasha in a kosher resort all summer.

Susie and Clarice slept on the side of the cabin that was closest to the bathroom. That was going to be very convenient because both of them were going to become world-class drinkers that summer. And they were both going to lose their virginity to much older men who worked at the resort and preyed on young, innocent women.

Mary-Ann and I had beds on the wall opposite Susie and Clarice's. Mary-Ann may or may not have been a virgin. She looked like a young Katharine Hepburn, and she told me that she was bisexual. Mary-Ann's cot and my cot were only a few inches apart. I wasn't a virgin, but I wasn't bisexual either. So, when Mary-Ann wasn't looking, I moved my bed a few more inches away. I didn't want to hurt her feelings.

1

Mary-Ann ended up with a man that summer anyway; a much older man named Louis. She would have been better off with someone who treated her better and who wasn't already balding, as would have Susie and Clarice. But that's neither here nor there. They paired off with their golf pros and health club managers and maître d's and didn't ask my opinion.

We were all cocktail waitresses at Hoffman's that summer in 1973. Most of us had never been away from home before, except to go to school. I had worked at a summer camp in the Catskills the previous summer and had gone to college in Boston the winter before.

I was a slender, but busty, long-legged, dark curly-haired, green-eyed girl from Long Island. I had been with plenty of young men and a few older ones. One was a tax attorney who gave me little gifts, like Snoopy pins and charm bracelets. He was one of the many men I had met at Hoffman's. I believe he was there for a singles weekend. But we weren't meant to be.

None of us were meant to be with who we were with that summer. We were just young women in training.

I ended up with a Jewish guy from Flatbush with a big Afro and a Brooklyn accent. His name was Mark Tallman. We were the real deal for a while, and I remember him fondly. On nights I didn't have to work in the nightclub or lounge, he and I worked back-stage together. He moved sets around, and I put makeup on comedians and singers, which is funny because I didn't wear any makeup personally and didn't know what the hell I was doing.

Mark and I had some good times together, and maybe we could have made it beyond the summer. But I was heading back to Boston in the fall, and he was heading elsewhere, and those were the years when settling down with one man didn't seem probable yet. I wasn't exactly run-around Sue (no offense to Susie), but I had a few wild oats to sow. And Mark tended to make women pregnant. Lots of women. So, that wasn't going to work for either one of us.

But that season was wonderful, even with all the caterwauling coming from the beds that were inches apart as we all brazenly engaged with our boys of summer. Apparently, we had no shame. It was great fun

2

until Rita showed up one day and scared us all straight with her wig and her age and her Rocco.

Rita didn't say much. She occupied the fifth bed in the cabin but never slept in it. She worked in the nightclub and the cocktail lounge, and then we guessed she took her earnings home to Rocco, wherever he was.

Sadly, she may have occasionally left with our tips in her wallet, but we didn't say anything because we were young and scared. We just stopped keeping our money in the chest of drawers between Clarice and Rita's beds. We were intimidated, but we weren't stupid. We worked hard for those tips, and, while we feared that Rita would get into trouble with her boyfriend if she didn't bring home a big score, we weren't working for our health. Far from it.

Hoffman's was an exciting place to work. It was a fun place to work. It was even a lucrative place to work. But it was not a healthy place to work. We got blood blisters on our feet and kidney infections and unplanned pregnancies. We all worked very long hours and staggered around in skimpy outfits and stilettos until the wee hours. We frequently went out for roast pork on garlic bread at 4 a.m. to wind down before hitting the sack as the sun rose. Whatever our condition, we all made it back to the cabin eventually.

Except for Rita. One day, she knocked off work and disappeared.

# CHAPTER 2

At first, we didn't know she was missing. After all, it wasn't like she was sleeping in the cabin. She came every afternoon with a paper sack containing her uniform, high heels, a toothbrush, and a makeup bag. We never saw a wig stand, but her hair was clearly not her own. Sometimes, the wig was on crooked. We never said anything. Rita was a woman of few words, and there was the Rocco thing to worry about. We just left her in peace and tried not to be having sex while she was present in the cabin. We knew she occasionally returned there before heading out to parts unknown in the middle of the night, but then a few days went by, and Rita never materialized. We asked our boss about it, but he just shrugged, and said, "People come and go around here. We'll find a replacement. Go back to work."

And we did as we were told because we had never developed a relationship with Rita, we thought we didn't have to worry about losing our tip money anymore, and we were busy getting laid. Rita was an anomaly around boy-crazed girls, and we didn't miss her for long because she was replaced by Sabra Chardonnay, an Israeli with wild strawberry hair and, I suspect, a made-up name, who was willing to let guys feel her up for a few extra bucks.

Sabra was a real hustler, and men were anxious to do all sorts of weird stuff with her in the cabin, which was a den of iniquity anyway. We didn't know what iniquity was until Sabra came onboard. There was a different guy there every afternoon. The nighttime was reserved for work, and none of us had the strength or enthusiasm to get crazy after hours. We were too busy unwinding over roast pork. Even Sabra passed out after a night of getting fondled by all the old lechers in the cocktail lounge and running up and down the long stairway leading to the service bar. She slept next to me on my side of the cabin, mostly on her stomach, with her long red curls cascading over the edge of the narrow bed.

Rita's bed remained empty for a while. Then, midsummer, a plump, rosy-cheeked, outspoken girl named Marsha showed up from Richmond, Virginia, and she had no choice but to take Rita's bed. I could have swapped with her. After all, Mary-Ann was bisexual, and I didn't care for her boyfriend. On the other hand, I had grown accustomed to my cot. It had a window behind it.

Marsha was soon involved with some Canadian guy named Johnny, and she was louder than most of us. It was better for her to be diagonally across the room. But Marsha and I ended up getting close. Even coming from Richmond, she knew what capon and kasha were all about. We had a little something in common culturally.

Speaking of capon and kasha, we all ate in a staff dining room, and it stayed open pretty late for breakfast so those of us on the night shift could get something to eat in the morning. Aside from roast pork.

At Hoffman's, you were able to get anything you wanted to eat, except for non-kosher food. For breakfast, that wasn't much of an issue, unless you were dying for bacon, which, considering the pork orgies we were having at the local diner at 4 a.m., we weren't. What we really needed was a little hydration.

Our waiter was a very heavy, sweaty man with rubbery lips and a crewcut named Leo. He liked me because I wasn't very demanding, and I smiled at him. He would approach me, and say, "Good morning, Mrs. Rockefeller. What would you like to drink? We have orange juice, apple juice, pineapple juice, grapefruit juice, prune juice, and sauerkraut juice. What is your pleasure?"

I would always have the same orange juice and a glass of water. Leo knew that, but he asked anyway. He liked to hear me giggle when he offered me sauerkraut juice. And, after I got finished laughing, and made my choice, he would follow up with, "Okay, Mrs. Rockefeller. Back to grim reality. What would you like to eat?" He knew, but always asked.

My roommates would always have something made with white bread and sugar, like French toast, while Marsha and I would have eggs or oatmeal.

One day, poor Leo lost it and ran across the dining room screaming, to no one in particular, "You don't care if I live or die! You don't care if I live or die!" We were very disturbed by this because we *did* care. We were somewhat comforted by the staff dining room manager who came in a minute later, and said, "If everyone in this room took their package and threw it into the middle of the room, everyone would leap for their own package."

Even at nineteen, we understood what he was saying. We knew what was in our packages. At nineteen, our packages were mostly empty. Leo clearly had a lot in his package. And when we thought about packages, something occurred to our underdeveloped minds: Rita had left without her package. We had taken her paper sack and its contents to our manager a few days after she disappeared and never gave it a second thought until the staff dining room manager made his speech about packages.

That's when we started to wonder if Rita was going to be found floating belly-up in the Hudson River. Without her wig. That was a sobering thought, and we brought it up with our boss.

"It's not your problem," he said. "Go back to work."

And we did.

But that's when a stranger showed up on our doorstep.

# CHAPTER 3

We were getting ready to go to work when a green Pontiac Firebird pulled up to the cabin. Most of us were crammed into the bathroom attempting to put on eyeliner, but Mary-Ann was kneeling on my bed looking out the window as the car crunched to a halt on the gravel. She yelled, "I think we have company," and we tumbled out of the bathroom like clowns out of a Volkswagen. At least we were all dressed.

A medium-sized, middle-aged man got out of the car. He looked down on what looked like a napkin and then peered at the window we were now all huddled around. We crashed into each other as we ducked out of view. We heard light footsteps on the stairs leading to the door, and then a tentative knock.

There were six of us and one of him, so Sabra told us all to spread out and shut up, and strode to the door. She flipped her hair back before opening it.

"Yeah?" she said.

The man had short dark hair and a thin mustache. His brown eyes looked huge behind his gold-rimmed glasses. He was wearing a tan leisure suit with an open-necked white shirt and a heavy gold cross on a thick chain. I was wondering if he was there for a singles weekend, but it was only Wednesday, and the cross wouldn't shout, "Choose me!" at a Hoffman's singles weekend. He seemed to be at a loss for words.

"Are you looking for someone?" asked Sabra in her Middle-Eastern-accented voice. She looked like she was ready to physically block him from entering the room.

"I'm Richard Lovato," he said. "Is this where the cocktail waitresses stay?"

We were all clustered behind Sabra wearing our slutty cocktail waitressing uniforms, so there was no denying it. We all collectively said, "Yes."

"I'm looking for Rita," he said.

Mary-Ann said, "We haven't seen Rita for a few days. Our boss told us to forget about it."

Much to all of our horror, the words came out, "Fuhgeddaboudit."

Lovato didn't seem to notice. He just nodded his head, and said, "I haven't seen her either. She was coming home very late, but she was coming home. Then, all of a sudden, she goes to work and doesn't come home."

"Does Rita call you Rocco by any chance?" asked Mary-Ann, timidly.

"Nah," said Lovato. 'I'm her cousin. Rita stays with me and my wife, Marie. She has a room at our house, over the garage. We help her out a little. She helps us out a little. You know, family stuff."

We all rolled our eyes when he mentioned Rita helping him and his wife out. We suspected that Rita was helping them out with our hard-earned dough, but we didn't say anything.

"May I ask what she does for your family?" asked Marsha.

"We have a sick kid," said Lovato. "She looks after him a coupla hours during the day while we work in our store. But Rita's got a life we don't know nothing about. Some guy gets her back and forth to work, but he don't come in the house. We don't know him. And now we don't know where Rita is."

Lovato touched the cross on his chest.

"How did you find us?" asked Sabra with her green eyes burning into Lovato's face.

"Rita told me she was gonna work here a coupla weeks during high season. After I found the place, I went up to some guys that were having a smoke outside one of the buildings and asked where the cocktail waitresses stay," he said. "Look. They drew me a map."

He showed us the napkin in his hand. It had the Hoffman's logo on it.

Marsha was incensed. She drawled, "They drew you a map? With what, chicken fat? Who the hell would send a strange man to our cabin? We're cocktail waitresses. We're not just any old waitresses. The hotel is supposed to be protecting us. That's why we sleep near the main building instead of out in left field with the other help."

She lifted up her hands and puffed to the universe, like she couldn't believe this was happening.

"All right," he said. "I'm not here to hurt nobody. I'm just looking for Rita. You don't know nothing, I can see that. Did she leave anything here?"

"You'll have to ask our boss about that," I said. "His name is George Ariti."

"Mr. Ariti will be in the cocktail lounge right now," I said. "He may still have Rita's stuff. We gave it to him after we were sure she was gone. In fact, we're all going to work right now. You can follow us. But first, Mr. Lovato, would you please write your name and number on that napkin so we can contact you if Rita shows up?"

He took a pen out of his shirt pocket and jotted down the information against the wall.

Rita, previously a person of little interest, was suddenly a person of great concern.

# CHAPTER 4

The Catskill Mountains are less than two hours north of New York City. Also known as the Borscht Belt and the Jewish Alps, the Catskills were my summer playground growing up. Those were happy times for my family. All those little white bungalows amid all the greenery, all the activities and entertainment, all those New York and Eastern European accents mingling over Mahjong. Multiple generations would go off to the country together to get away from the heat of cities and suburbs. I was exposed from birth to the joys of the Catskill summer. What was familiar to me had to be appallingly foreign to most of the women I shared the cabin with.

"What's a shiksa?" Susie asked me one day.

"It's a gentile woman," I replied. "Why?"

"Some guy yelled at me the other day, 'Hey, shiksa, come open my wine bottle.' Why would he be so rude?"

"Exuberance," I said. "Don't take it as an insult. You won't find too much gentility around here. Some guy called *me* a shiksa just because I carry booze on my tray instead of stuffed cabbage."

Susie looked puzzled, but over the summer she was going to learn that Hoffman's guests were full of loud excitement. Having shed the shackles of the Old Country, they felt free, well-fed, and unpersecuted. They were surrounded by their own kind, and everybody spoke the same language. Loudly. And joyfully. They felt entitled and didn't mind talking down to the servants.

We all worked out of a service bar for a foreman named Jules. He loved Susie and hated me, probably because I had curly hair like he did. There was no other explanation that I could imagine because I was a fine, hard-working waitress. On the other hand, the service bartender loved everyone, especially me. Probably because I was a lightweight. Bill was always trying out weird new drink concoctions on me, just to see if I turned green. The drinks didn't make me sick, but his sexual innuendos did. I forgave him because he never laid a hand on me.

And then there was George Ariti, our very proper and soft-spoken boss. He treated us all with paternal respect, and only asked us to do our jobs.

Right now, he looked up from whatever he was working on when we entered the cocktail lounge with Richard Lovato in tow. His gaze was calm and vaguely curious.

"Who is this?" he asked.

"He's Rita's cousin, Richard Lovato," I said.

"Nice to meet you, Mr. Lovato," said Ariti. "Do you live around here?"

"Yeah," said Lovato. "I run a general store in Ellenville."

"Ah," said Lovato. "Do you have news of your cousin?"

"Nah," said Lovato. "That's why I'm here. Rita doesn't come home a coupla days, I'm okay with that. She needs to have a life. She don't get much privacy at home. But it's been more than a coupla days now. She don't come home, and she don't call. That's not like her. Plus, my wife has had to stay home with our son instead of helping me at the store. Rita got a mother in Jersey, but she don't go there no more, and I don't talk to her mother either."

Ariti said "I'm very sorry to hear that, Mr. Lovato. Rita came in for her pay on Sunday. I gave her cash, as she requested. She never returned. No explanation."

Lovato shook his head. "I came here for answers but it sounds like you're as much in the dark as I am."

"What do you know about her boyfriend?" asked Ariti.

"His name is Rocco, and I think he lives in Monticello. Maybe he likes to play the horses. Rita never introduced me to the guy. Don't ask me why."

Ariti nodded sympathetically, and said, "I have her belongings in my office, if you can show me some form of identification. Had she given me contact information, I would have called you when she didn't show up for work. We have a lot of transients working here, Mr. Lovato. She responded to an ad for a cocktail waitressing job, and we were short on staff so I thought I'd give her a shot. She said she had waitressing experience. I felt

11

bad for her. She seemed like a sweet woman down on her luck, you know? Desperate."

"She's family, but she keeps a lot to herself. Not a big talker. Now I'm worried."

Ariti said, "I think a call to the authorities is in order. I'm happy to speak to the police but there's not much I can tell them. As I said, people are in and out of here all the time."

Mary-Ann said to Ariti, "You told us that someone was picking Rita up and dropping her off. Did you see what he was driving? Was it Rocco? When did the car stop showing up?"

"I think he was driving some kind of Ford. And he stopped showing up when Rita went missing. I couldn't tell you if it was Rocco or not. Like I said, I never met the guy."

"And I was never around when Rita got dropped off," I said. "She always just seemed to be in the cabin when I showed up to get ready for work."

I looked around and asked my roommates if any of them had ever seen Rita show up. They all shook their heads.

I asked Ariti, "Are there cameras by the front gate?"

"Good question, Amy," said Ariti. "I'll have our security guys look into it and turn over whatever they find to the police. Mr. Lovato, I will need your contact information. Girls, anything else?"

We all stood there shuffling our feet. We were truly clueless. I barely remembered a single conversation that I'd had with Rita, and I've got a good memory.

Clarice piped up, and said, "Rita wore a wig."

Lovato lifted his eyebrows, and said, "What for? She got plenty of hair."

We all did a collective shrug.

"Let me go get her stuff," said Ariti. "Girls, get to work."

I kept Lovato's napkin to myself, just in case I had any reason to contact him directly. You never know.

# CHAPTER 5

There was a fireman's convention in town, so we all made out well that night. With the usual guests, you were lucky if you sold an occasional glass of scotch with a hefty splash of water. The firemen drank like there was no tomorrow, and they were good tippers. So, we merrily ran and up and down the stairs to the service bar to fill large alcohol orders and delivered them to boisterous, but polite, men. Before the night was out, we were all on a first-name basis.

Bill the bartender was down in the service bar, working like a Trojan. His head appeared to be detached from his body as he leered at us and sometimes wiggled his tongue as his hands performed miracles with drinks. He could have been blind and still gotten all the orders straight.

We cocktail waitresses were required to carry dozens of drinks on small cork-and-plastic trays over our heads. The shots were separate from mixers, so you needed to be able to identify the difference between rye and gin in a dark nightclub and mix drinks in front of customers without dropping anything. When I first started, I foolishly attempted to balance a tray on the edge of a table, and the entire order landed on the floor. Another time, I accidentally dropped a shot of vodka down singer Vic Damone's neck. He was very gracious about it.

We used our arms and legs to get chairs back under tables as soon as parties left to quickly prepare setups for the next group. We were all constantly running in our heels, kicking and maneuvering, putting down and picking up, smiling and wiping, calculating tabs, and sometimes reminding people to tip if they liked our service. We were only being paid $1.12 an hour by the hotel. Tips were our life blood, and we completely knocked ourselves out to earn them.

That's why it hurt to see them disappear when we finally settled down for a few hours of sleep.

Rita. Was she really running off with our money and then coming back for more? Did she think we weren't noticing that our tips were gone

13

when she left the cabin? Or were we accusing her unjustly? When we fell in at 5 a.m., after a long shift and pork, did we always remember to lock the door before passing out? Maybe not. There were plenty of unsavory characters around – ex-cons and opportunists and perverts, oh my.

When the last person left the nightclub, I approached Ariti and asked if he had learned any more from Lovato. He said, "No, and I don't want any of you girls to get mixed up in this mess. This woman came to us out of the blue, worked less than a couple of weeks, and disappeared. From what you girls tell me, she never even slept here. She ran home to her cousin in the middle of the night, which sounds strange to me. And the cousin never met her boyfriend? Why not? What's the big secret?"

"I don't know what to think, Mr. Ariti," I said.

I was debating whether to tell him about the missing tips, but decided not to. Not yet anyway.

"The cousin told me that Rita had a mother in New Jersey, but he didn't speak with her either," said Ariti. "I think he'd better get over it and give her a call. If Rita's there, fine. If she's not, he needs to get the police involved."

I nodded.

"I know you girls talk, but try not to spread any of this around outside of the cabin," said Mr. Ariti. "You're all young girls, and part of my job is to protect you."

"I understand, Mr. Ariti."

"On the other hand, if something slides out from under a bed that could cast some light on the matter – a letter, or whatever – please let me know. Just come straight to me, and don't discuss it with anyone else. I don't need to get this hotel embroiled in a scandal."

"I understand, Mr. Ariti."

I left Ariti, and went running off to join the other girls at the Mountaintop Café. We were going to pass on the pork and have egg foo young instead. Bill and some of the apprentice bartenders were going to be there, too.

Clarice begged off. Her stomach felt queasy. She thought she would head back to the cabin and get some sleep. That's what we all should have done. We were physically dragging ass after a night with the firemen, but,

14

mentally, we were wired.  We parted ways with Clarice at the fork in the road – one that led down to the Mountaintop and one that led to the cabin.

We had a couple of drinks with our egg foo young and had a few laughs with the bartenders. We were all creatures of the night. Soon, the sun would come up, and we'd all burst into flames. It was time to call it a day and head back to our cabin.

Our eyes were half-closed, and we were stumbling over our own feet, but there was one thing we couldn't miss when we opened the door and turned on the light. Clarice was nowhere to be found.

# CHAPTER 6

A nd then there were five," Sabra muttered under her breath.

"Knock it off, Sabra," said Mary-Ann. "This isn't a laughing matter."

Susie ran wild-eyed through the cabin calling Clarice's name. When she finished searching the bathroom and closet and the floor under each bed, she looked at all of us, one face at a time, and yelled, "Where the hell is Clarice?", as if we knew.

"We saw her, the same as you did," said Marsha. "She was heading back to the cabin when we went to the Mountaintop. She wasn't feeling well, remember?"

"Damnit," said Susie, as she sat on her bed, "I knew I shouldn't have let her go back alone. What was I thinking?"

"It wasn't more than a two-hundred-foot walk from where we parted," I said.

"Yeah, but she had to go past the kitchen where all those creepy dishwashers hang out," said Mary-Ann.

"The dishwashers have a night shift and a day shift. It would be easy enough to find out who was on duty at that hour," I said.

"Who's in charge of the dishwashers?" Marsha asked.

"Gordie. But he wouldn't personally be here at 4 a.m. I don't even know when he comes in."

"I think we have to let someone know right away," I said. "But maybe she just met up with her boyfriend for an early breakfast. He's a golf pro and up at the crack of dawn before hitting the course. He knows when she gets off. Maybe he surprised her at the cabin and invited her to join him. She could come home any minute."

I looked out the window behind my bed as if I were expecting to see Denny's car pulling up. Trees were in silhouette across the lightening sky. There was nothing out there, unless someone was hiding in the shadows.

Mary-Ann asked Susie, "Is Clarice one to play some kind of sick joke?"

Susie stared at her like she was out of her mind.

Mary-Ann continued, "I mean, first Rita disappears, and we don't give it much thought until her cousin shows up and tells us he doesn't know where she is either. Then we find out that she's taking care of his sick kid during the day. Then we go to Mr. Ariti, and he tells us this place is chock full of transients and that we should keep our noses out of everything. And then Clarice disappears on the same day? Seriously? Something is rotten here."

"That's an understatement," I said. "I wish we had a phone in this cabin. We need to get a hold of a security guard. Surely they have at least one patrolling the grounds at night, right?"

"There should be one walking us all back to our cabin in the dark," said Marsha. "If there are any, they're probably off protecting the guests. I've never seen one."

"Well, we need to band together and find one right now," I said.

"I don't want to go," said Sabra. "I don't know what kind of creep is hanging around out there."

"You stay here then and get your beauty rest," I said. "The rest of us are going out to either find Clarice or a security guard, whichever comes first."

"Make sure you don't first run into an ax murderer," said Sabra.

"If we do, we'll send him to you," I said.

"I would have thought you would have been the bravest of us," said Mary-Ann to Sabra.

"Hey, I'm here to make money," said Sabra. "It's not part of my job to track down missing persons and put my own life at risk. I didn't know Rita at all and I barely know Clarice. Ariti wouldn't want us involved."

"And yet, we are," I said. "Let's go, girls.

To Sabra, I added, "Better lock the door behind us."

—

It was pretty light by the time we marched out of the cabin, four women in cocktail waitress uniforms and tennis shoes. We didn't know how far we were going to have to walk to find help. And we didn't know if we were

17

going to have to run for our lives. We had no idea of what we were going to run into, and none of us wanted to stumble upon our friend's body, or anyone else's.

"Clarice had better not be screwing with us," said Mary-Ann.

Susie, who knew her better than we did, said, "Clarice would never do something like that. She's from Dallas."

"Yeah," I said. "Mary-Ann would be a lot more likely to pull something like that. She's from the Cape."

We all chuckled a little to break the tension. That, and we hadn't run into anyone with a bloody ax yet. We just quickly walked the gravel path that led to the main hotel building. We did not pass any dishwashers on our way. We were relieved to see someone manning the front desk.

"What are you girls doing here?" asked the woman with a name tag on her uniform pocket. Her name was Betty. "Didn't the cocktail lounge shut down hours ago?"

"Yes," I said. "We went to the Mountaintop after shift, but one of us went back to the cabin instead because she was feeling under the weather. When we got home about an hour later, she wasn't there. We need to report her as missing. Is there a security guard here?"

"Oh, goodness," said Betty. "Yes, Mike should be out there patrolling. He always walks the halls and the periphery of the guest quarters."

"But not the servants' quarters?" Marsha sneered.

Betty gave Marsha a cold look, and said, "Look, we have thousands of guests here, thirty-five buildings, and twelve-hundred acres of land. It's a full-time job for Mike."

"From what I understand," I said, "there are also about a thousand employees. Sounds like a lot of territory for Mike."

Betty said, "He has a couple of assistants. But I agree with you, there should be more. Sometimes people get into trouble. You know, we've got a diverse population here, and the management has given lots of people second chances in life."

"So, there are some ex-cons here, right?" said Marsha.

18

Betty looked at Marsha for a long moment, and finally said, "Yes, we have a few. We have the occasional incident, but they mostly behave themselves."

I could just imagine a dance instructor or some guy who runs the bingo game going berserk on a guest, but I kept my thoughts to myself.

"Whatever," I said. "Clarice O'Hare is missing, and we are reporting her absence. Please call someone now. She's only been gone an hour or I would suggest calling the police. She may still show up, but we don't know that. So please contact Mike right away."

We watched her pick up a walkie-talkie from behind the desk. It squawked when she pressed the talk button.

"Yeah?" came a man's voice.

"Mike, this is Betty at the front desk."

"Yeah?"

"I have four cocktail waitresses here who have told me that one of their roommates has gone missing."

"Yeah? Since when?"

"Since earlier this morning. They don't know if she ever made it back to the cabin after work."

"I'll be right there," said Mike. "Tell the girls to wait."

We were dead on our feet but were afraid that Clarice could be literally dead, or worse. So, we sprawled out on a couple of couches in the lobby to await the arrival of Mike the security guard. He was there before we could even release a sigh of exhaustion. And he was with Ariti.

# CHAPTER 7

Ariti had clearly not been to bed yet. He was still in his suit and crisp white shirt, looking fresh as a daisy. His thick, wavy, black hair looked varnished. There was a frown on his face as he approached us and a concerned look in his sad eyes.

Before Mike could say a word, Ariti said, "What's going on, girls?"

I said, "We went down to the Mountaintop after work, without Clarice. She didn't feel well and begged off. She told us she was going back to the cabin, but she wasn't there when we got home. That's the long and short of it."

Ariti ran his hands over his face and pressed his fingers into the area over his eyes.

"What's going on, Mr. Ariti?" Mike asked. "You told me just yesterday that another woman in your employ went missing a few days ago, and now this?"

"You know that people come and go here, Mike," said Ariti. "With the first one, I figured she just took her money and split. It's been known to happen. I didn't think anything about it until her cousin showed up yesterday, making inquiries. Clarice is another matter. She's a young girl and a good kid. She's been here since the beginning of the summer. This I take seriously from the get-go."

Mike asked us, "Did you notice anything amiss when you got to the cabin? Was her bed slept in? Did you see any signs of a struggle?"

Marsha said, "We didn't stick around very long to investigate. We just noticed she wasn't there and came right here."

"I know you girls must be tired, but I'm going to have to go back to the cabin with you and have a look around," said Mike. "I'm not supposed to get the authorities involved until she's been missing for twenty-four hours, but considering that another one of you ladies disappeared within the past few days, I would have to say we have a situation here. Let's first see if she's returned to the cabin."

"Keep me apprised, Mike," said Ariti.

At that moment, I suspected that Ariti never left the hotel.

By the time we followed Mike down the path to our cabin, the sun was making its way up, and it already felt like a hot day. Mike knew where our cabin was, and he walked up the steps ahead of us as if he had a key. Turns out, he did. He let himself in and saw Sabra out cold on her cot.

"That's not Clarice, is it?" he asked.

Mary-Ann said, "No, that's Sabra. She didn't want to get involved. She needed her beauty rest. Clarice's bed is over there," she said pointing it out.

Sabra stirred and mumbled, "What's happening?"

"Nothing that would concern you," said Marsha.

Sabra rolled over and faced the wall, lifting the sheet over her shoulder.

Mike went over to Clarice's bed and observed without touching anything. He told us, "Girls, this may be a crime scene, so just stand back. Do you see anything that looks different?

I felt like saying, "Yeah, there's a great, big pool of blood in the middle of the room with Clarice's name written in it," but I didn't.

Nothing looked disturbed, yet something seemed off. The bed was made and had clearly not been slept in. There was no head dent in the pillow, no uniform hastily thrown on the floor, no jewelry on the nightstand. My head went in circles trying to figure out what I was missing. It would have gone in circles anyway after a twelve-hour shift and two drinks at 4 a.m., but concern was sharpening my senses.

Marsha was watching me.

"What are you thinking, Amy?" she asked.

I stared at the bed and its environs for a few more seconds.

And then I looked at our uniforms. We were wearing the red miniskirts tonight, not the baby-blue ones. We had all taken off our shoes to change into sneakers before heading over to the hotel. Red high heels were tucked under all of our beds.

Including Clarice's.

"The shoes," I said. "Those were the shoes she wore tonight. She was here."

Mike said, "Did she have more than one pair?"

I looked at Susie, and said, "Susie? Did she?"

"I doubt it," Susie said. "Those shoes are pricey. And it's not like we have lots of space to put our stuff. We all know what we've got. Let's go check the closet and see if we come up with an extra pair. Clarice is skinny, but she wears a size nine shoe."

We asked Mike if Susie could enter the closet and check. He nodded, and we waited.

"Try not to disturb anything," he said.

Susie walked into the closet and began to examine Clarice's one-sixth of it.

"I see sneakers and flip flops. No high heels, except blue ones," she called out.

"Call the cops," I said to Mike. "I think that Clarice left here barefoot."

# CHAPTER 8

Mike told us to try to get a little sleep. He was going to get one of his assistants to sit on our porch and keep an eye on the cabin until the police got there, and every day after that.

"You probably have a couple of hours for a little shut-eye," he said. "Mr. Ariti and I will meet with the police at the hotel first."

"As if we'll be able to sleep," Marsha said, eyeballing Sabra's back. "When will you get your assistant here, and what's his name in case we need to scream it?" she asked.

"I'll send Charlie over," said Mike. "He's a good guy. He's been a part of the hotel family for a long time, and I trust him."

Mike got on his walkie-talkie and, at the squawk, said, "Charlie?"

"Yeah?"

"Mike, here. Get over to the cocktail waitress' cabin, on the double."

"Trouble there?" Charlie asked.

"Could be. I need you to watch over the place for a while."

"You gonna tell me what's going on there?" asked Charlie.

"One of the girls has gone missing, as of early this morning. We're calling the cops. But I need to get to the main building, and Drew's on day shift. You just need to sit on a folding chair, and keep your eyes and ears open for a couple of hours."

"10-4," said Charlie. "On the way. Over and out."

Mike told us he would wait until Charlie arrived before he headed off. Morning was fully upon us, along with breakfast aromas from the kitchen. We were usually asleep at this hour, oblivious to early stirrings of Catskill hotel activities, like Simon Says, calisthenics on the big lawn, and guys in plaid Bermuda shorts teeing off on the golf course. That reminded me. Clarice's boyfriend, Denny, was a golf pro at Hoffman's.

Denny was blonde, tan, and middle-aged, with shocking blue eyes, a florid complexion, and the beginnings of a paunch. He was always dressed in pastels and never wore shorts of any kind. With his lank yellow hair and pink pants, he reminded me of the Easter Bunny out there on the links. If the Easter Bunny wore pants.

I said to Mike, "When you go, you may want to check out Denny the golf pro. Clarice was dating him."

"Really?" he asked.

"Yup."

"Well, what's a little girl like Clarice want with an old buck like Denny?"

"Why don't you ask her when you find her?" I said.

Susie said, "Denny's not so bad. I'm seeing an older man, too, and he treats me very nicely."

"Have you seen the two of them together?" asked Mike.

"Sure, I have," said Susie. "We've double-dated a couple of times, when we have the rare night off. They seemed okay. He might have been a little possessive."

"How did that play out?" asked Mike.

"Well, if we were sitting in a restaurant and another guy gave her the eye, he would put his hand on her wrist and chill the other guy out. Like that."

"Doesn't sound overly aggressive," said Mike. "But we will definitely go down to the golf club and have a talk with Denny the golf pro."

Just then, Charlie showed up looking like a strong wind could blow him over. He seemed to be weighed down by his walkie-talkie. But he also carried a firearm. Wow – this was getting serious."

Mike handed us off to Charlie, after we handed Charlie the one folding chair in the cabin, and we locked the door behind us. If Charlie needed to get in, he was going to have to bang on the door or go grab Mike. Unless he, too, had a key.

Suddenly, Sabra was awake and very chatty. She turned to face us and hoisted her head on her hand, with her elbow bent.

"What's the scoop?" she asked.

Mary-Ann said, "You didn't hear any of that? We weren't making any effort to keep our voices down. It would appear that Clarice was back here before she left, maybe without her shoes."

24

"Whaddya talking about?" asked Sabra. "She left without her shoes?"

"She left without her *work* shoes," I said. "And her sneakers and flip flops are in the closet."

"Did anyone take Clarice's shoes to check for evidence?" asked Sabra.

All of a sudden, Sabra was very involved.

"The police will be coming by pretty soon," I said. "There's a guard outside the door, and he's going to stay there until the cops show up. I think we'd better get used to it because I think we're going to have a guard on our doorstep for the rest of the summer, night and day."

"Oh, man," said Sabra. "There goes my sex life."

"I think you'll figure it out," said Marsha. "We're already having a time coordinating our sex lives."

"Yeah, but your sex lives won't get you arrested in forty-seven states," said Sabra with a straight face.

"Go back to sleep, Sabra," Marsha said.

We were all ready to catch a few minutes of Zs, but we needed to put that night's tips away before going to bed. We were back to stashing our money in the bureau again. We only got to the bank once a week, when we hopped on a jitney that brought us into town with our sacks of dough. There were a lot of ones and fives in there.

But Marsha was the first to take her cash to the drawer, and what she saw made her yell.

"Goddamnit," she shrieked while throwing underwear out of the dresser. "Someone has taken off with my money again!"

# CHAPTER 9

We were awakened mid-morning by a knock on the door.
"Girls," someone who sounded like Ariti said. "It's George Ariti. Are you decent?"

"We were asleep," yelled Mary-Ann, who had the bed closest to the door. Please give us a minute, Mr. Ariti."

"You can stay in bed," he said. "Just cover yourselves. I have two policeman with me."

We did as we were told, and Mary-Ann called out, "The door is locked. Do you have a key?"

"Yes," said Ariti. "We keep duplicates of all keys in the main building. Can we enter?"

"We all looked at each other to get silent agreement, then nodded at our spokesperson, Mary-Ann.

"Yes," she said. "You can come in now."

We heard the key turning in the lock, and Ariti entered first, looking shy. Two officers followed him in, one middle-aged and one young. They were in uniform and had all sorts of paraphernalia hanging from their belts, including handcuffs, nightsticks, and guns. Tools of the trade. Mike came in behind them. But that was the end of it. Charlie was apparently sent home.

Suddenly, the cabin seemed way too small. None of them looked like they wanted to be there, except for the younger cop who gave us all a big smile.

"Good morning, ladies," said the older cop. "I am Officer Ed Wiley with the Liberty Police. And this is Officer Ryan Parker. I'm sorry to wake you up this way, but I have something important to discuss with you."

I could feel us all bracing ourselves for what was coming next. Wiley took off his hat and looked down into it, as if he were looking for words there.

"First, I want to thank you for reporting your co-worker's absence this morning. She has been found, and she's been hospitalized."

Susie let out a gasp.

Wiley continued, "I cannot discuss her injuries with you at this time. What I can tell you is that her parents have been informed. They will pick her up after we have finished the preliminaries of this investigation. And then, she will be returning to Dallas to recuperate with her family."

We were all stricken silent, except for Susie who was weeping, and Wiley continued to address us.

"I understand that another waitress went missing from this cabin a few days ago."

"Rita disappeared," volunteered Marsha, sitting up and tugging the sheet above her chest. "We thought she was taking our tips, but now we're not so sure."

"What's this about taking your tips?" asked Ariti.

"We didn't want to say anything because we were afraid of her boyfriend, but that's neither here nor there now," said Marsha.

"When did you discover that your money was missing?" asked Wiley.

"When we got back from reporting Clarice missing," I said. "Marsha went to put her money in the drawer where we normally keep it until we can get into town to bank it, and she told us that all of our money was gone."

There were a couple of bras still lying on the floor from Marsha's frantic underwear toss.

Mary-Ann gave Sabra a look, and said, "Did you have a quickie with one of your slime balls while we were out giving Mr. Ariti the news about Clarice?"

"I went to sleep, you skinny bitch," came the reply. "And the door was locked. Nobody came in, and nobody went out, as far as I know."

The two women glared at each other. Ariti put a hand out, and said, "Knock it off," in his soft but commanding voice. Mary-Ann and Sabra both crossed their arms and fell back against their headboards.

Mike said, "We have multiple crimes going on around here, Ed."

Mike and Wiley were on a first-name basis. The young cop had still not said a word but was staring at Sabra's pouting profile.

"I can see that," said Wiley.

"What is our next step, Officer Wiley?" asked Ariti.

"Is there anything else you would like to tell me, ladies?" Wiley asked, looking each of us in the eyes.

"Yes," I said. "Clarice was here before she got into trouble because we noticed her shoes under her bed when we got in. We suspect she may have been barefoot when she left this cabin."

"That is consistent with our findings," said Wiley.

"And her boyfriend is the golf pro, Denny Martin," added Marsha.

"Yes, we have already spoken with Mr. Martin," said Wiley. "If there's nothing more, I would like all of you to get up and get dressed. Try not to touch anything. Pack a bag, and don't leave any valuables behind. You're going to the big house."

"What the hell?" yelled Sabra. "You're taking us to jail?"

"No," said Ariti. "He means the main house. I've arranged a family suite for all of you for the next two or three days. Just until the police have thoroughly investigated this cabin and environs. There are two queen-sized beds and two singles in the suite. There's also a nice bathroom with a big tub. You'll like it."

Sabra asked, "Can't I just shack up with one of my boyfriends at the waiters' quarters?"

Wiley winced a little, and said, "Miss, there will be no shacking up. You will stay at the hotel and not leave the premises until I have cleared you to do so."

Susie said she would share a bed with Mary-Ann, and I said I would share a bed with Marsha. Sabra could have a single or two for herself. We would manage for the few days.

"Should we bring our uniforms and shoes with us?" Mary-Ann asked.

"Of course, bring them," said Ariti. "It's going to be business as usual. But we are going to put your earnings in the safe in my office until we can bring you to the bank."

Wiley warned us not to touch anything around Clarice's bed and to leave any of her belongings undisturbed. We did have to tell him that one of the bras on the floor was hers, and we also told him how it got there.

"Make it fast ladies," he said, leading the men toward the door. "We don't want this case cooling down on us. Your safety is our top priority."

We believed him.

# CHAPTER 10

Clarice had seen Denny before her shift. He had swung by in his red Cadillac Coupe de Ville, and they had taken a ride in the country. Clarice sat quietly in the passenger seat while Denny fidgeted with the radio dial. Clarice was naturally quiet, but she had something to say. She groped for the right words. Finally, she spat out, "I think I may be pregnant." Denny's hand froze on the dial.

He slowed the car down and pulled off to the side of the road. Traffic was light on Route 17 that afternoon. The car ticked like a time bomb after he turned the ignition key to the off position, cooling down. It was a hot day, and the air conditioner had been cranked up high. They sat in silence for a moment, and then Denny exploded, "What?"

"I've been throwing up a lot," said Clarice.

"You're a skinny girl," said Denny. "Maybe there's something else wrong with you."

"I don't think so," said Clarice. "This has only been since you made me have sex with you."

"That was weeks ago," Denny roared. "How was I supposed to know you were a virgin? And I didn't force you to do anything. You told me you were ready."

"I guess I wasn't," said Clarice. "Why did you have to be so rough?"

"You thought that was rough? There was nothing rough about it. You were just so limp."

"It was rough for a first time, Denny. I didn't know what I was getting into."

"Well, it's been a while since I've been with a virgin. Who the hell is a virgin at nineteen these days? I mean it's 1973, for Christ's sake."

"Well, I think I'm pregnant now," said Clarice.

"Yeah, you told me," said Denny. "What do you want me to do about it?"

"Marry me, maybe."

"Marry you, no way. Even if I didn't have a wife in White Plains, I wouldn't marry you."

"You have a wife?"

"Yeah, and two kids."

"Why aren't they up here with you for the summer?"

"My wife is a lawyer in White Plains, and the kids go to day camp there. They come up for a weekend now and then."

"I've never seen them."

"You think we stay here when they come? Hey, I need a change of scenery, too. We usually head to the Amish country. But that's none of your concern."

Clarice started to cry, "You told me that you love me."

"Hey, I would have said anything to get to you, honey. Man, you're a dumb kid. What a baby you are."

Clarice looked out the window with tears streaming down her face.

"Take me back to the hotel," she said.

Denny turned the car back on, checked the side-view and rear-view mirrors, and got back on the road.

"Speaking of babies, he said, "what are you going to do about the kid? I mean, provided that you're actually pregnant?"

"What do you mean, what am I going to do? I'm a Catholic. I'm going to have it."

"I'm a Catholic, too, but you're going to have to get rid of that kid. No kidding, Clarice, I'll give you the money. I don't want to hear any more talk about you keeping that kid."

He looked at her, but she continued to look at the trees whizzing by her window.

"Are you listening to me?" he said.

Clarice turned to him, and said, "I hear you Denny, you son of a bitch."

Denny reared back, and said, "Nice talk from a Catholic girl."

"I'm going to have this baby, Denny, and I will make sure your wife knows about it. When my father finds out about this, he'll come gunning for you. Bet on it."

"You're threatening me now?" Denny yelled.

31

"What options are you giving me?" asked Clarice. "I won't have an abortion."

Denny stopped the car in the middle of the empty road, shifted in his seat, and punched Clarice twice in the stomach. Hard. When she doubled over, he squeezed her face in his hand, and said, "Maybe you're not so pregnant anymore," and he threw her head against the back of the seat.

Clarice sat in stunned silence, holding her belly. Her jaw felt out of joint. When Denny stopped in front of the cabin, he said, "Get out, and keep your mouth shut."

Clarice slowly opened the car door and made her way up the steps. Denny sped off before she got her key out. When she entered the cabin, nobody was there. She went into the bathroom to urinate and discovered she was bleeding. She put on a sanitary napkin and got up to look in the mirror. Deep purple bruises were already ringing the lower half of her face. She opened the medicine cabinet and took out a jar of concealer, which she put on her nightstand.

Sitting on the edge of her bed, Clarice pulled her tank top over her head. Her neck was stiff, limiting her movements. She was going to have to get her uniform on before she applied the concealer. She didn't want to mess up her top. She also didn't want to have to change in front of the other girls who would be back in the cabin very soon.

Clarice wadded up her blood-stained underpants and threw them in the trash can under the bathroom sink. She grimaced as she put on clean underwear and a red miniskirt. Her stomach felt like something had ruptured inside. She wondered how she was going to be able to stand straight in stilettos. She took a hand mirror from the nightstand and applied the concealer, just before the other girls got home.

"Hey, Clarice," said Susie when she entered the room. "You missed a great day at the lake. We all went canoeing! How was your ride with Denny?"

"It was nice," said Clarice, looking up from her bed and giving Susie a smile. "We saw lots of cows," she said, laughing.

Clarice's face was bigger than the rest of her. At some point, she would have a frog neck. For now, she was a slim girl with good teeth and soft brown eyes.

"You're ready early," said Mary-Ann. "We're all going to have to hustle. Just enough time for a quick shower. I've got to wash off all this iodine and baby oil."

"No wonder you're so tan," I said. You're marinating yourself before getting out into the sun."

"You know it," she said, grinning.

The girls got dressed and made up their faces, except for me – I only applied makeup on entertainers. We all took off to the main house together, hobbling on our red heels, especially Clarice who seemed to be walking more slowly than usual. She could barely keep up.

"Are you all right?" I asked, looking back.

"Oh, I'm fine," she said. "I just have a little bit of a bellyache. My period just started."

"Are you fit to work a twelve-hour shift?"

"I think so. I don't want to miss the fireman's convention. I hear that's good money. Those guys can really drink."

"So I've heard," I said. "Most of the rest of our customers drink seltzer with a twist of lime. We need those firemen."

Clarice nodded.

"If you really start to feel lousy, cash out, and go back to the cabin," I said.

"I will," said Clarice.

# CHAPTER 11

Clarice parted with the other women and made her way down the gravel path, stumbling with exhaustion. Both pockets of her skirt bulged with bills. It had been a good night, especially in the cocktail lounge. That's where most of the firemen ended up. The usual guests were in the nightclub, nursing ginger ales. She hurt from head to toe. She took her shoes off and stepped off the path onto the grass, which was a lot more comfortable on her aching feet. She didn't have far to go. She looped two fingers into the fronts of her pumps so that they dangled from her hands.

It was still dark out, but the path was lit with one tall street lamp, and there were lights on in the back of the kitchen. When Clarice passed, she heard the usual litany of "Chocha chocha, mamacita," from hidden faces. She vaguely saw the shadows of skinny men in white t-shirts, smoking cigarettes. She shook her head and continued toward the cabin. The waitresses heard this idiocy emanating from the back of the kitchen all the time. They always just kept on walking until the dishwashers were out of sight and earshot.

Suddenly, someone grabbed her from behind. She tried to call out, but the attacker had one hand around her throat and the other around her mouth. She couldn't breathe and started to lose consciousness. The shoes fell from her hands as she was shoved toward the woods. She began to fall. Her attacker allowed her to drop and dragged her a short distance. Clarice couldn't have weighed more than a hundred pounds, and she slid easily over the brush.

Clarice was deposited under a tree, face up. Whoever had assaulted her went right for her pockets, removing her money and key. It was too dark to see the blood coursing down Clarice's legs as she lay in a shallow indentation beside a red pine. The assailant searched for jewelry and removed Clarice's watch before abandoning her in the forest. Finding Clarice's shoes near the path, the assailant picked them up and brought them up the stairs to the cabin.

—

The police found Clarice in the woods the next morning. The concealer had worn off, so her facial bruises were immediately apparent, and a large amount of blood had stained the pine straw that she lay in. Her head was turned at a strange angle. At first, they thought she was dead.

One of the cops gently touched her shoulder and was startled when she opened her eyes. The older of the two policemen told her not to move and that she was safe.

"Looks like you've had a rough night, miss," he said. "I'm Officer Ed Wiley, and this is my partner, Officer Ryan Parker. "You're going to be all right now. Can you tell me your name?"

Clarice's throat felt dry. She stared at Wiley for a moment before whispering, "Clarice O'Hare."

"Do you have any recall of what happened to you?" asked Wiley.

Clarice tried to nod, but her stiff neck wouldn't allow it. She said, "I was walking home, and someone grabbed me from behind."

"Did you see who it was?"

"No."

"I don't want to sound indelicate, Clarice, but you've bled pretty badly. Were you sexually assaulted?"

"I don't know," said Clarice, her eyes filling with tears.

"Is it your time of the month?"

"I don't know."

"You have some bruises on your face, and you seem to be in some pain with your neck. Did this happen during the attack?"

Clarice closed her eyes, blocking everything out.

Wiley said, "That's okay, Clarice. We have an ambulance on the way. There's no need to answer any more questions now. We're just happy that we found you safe. You're going to be okay. Just rest a little before the ambulance shows up. We'll get to the bottom of this later."

Just then, an ambulance came down the path with its siren turned off. No need to alarm the guests. Its wheels straddled the grass on both sides of the gravel walkway. Two EMTs emerged with a stretcher and other medical paraphernalia. They stabilized Clarice's neck and carefully lifted her from the ground.

When the ambulance departed, the police contacted Mike the security guard, and Mike contacted Ariti. They all met in front of the cabin.

It was time to wake the girls.

# CHAPTER 12

Staying at the hotel was a luxury for all of us. We were in no hurry to get back to the cabin. For one thing, the beds were big and comfortable, even if we had to share them. And no guys were allowed in the suite, so we had more privacy than we were accustomed to. Sabra was the only one who bitched about what she called "our confinement." I didn't feel that confined, even with old Charlie sitting outside our door all night and Drew all day. Drew was the other assistant security guard, a recent hire, and he was pretty hunky. Sabra was already giving him the eye and who knew what else while our backs were turned.

After the third day, Ariti told us we were going back to the cabin, with heightened surveillance.

"The police have gone through the cabin very thoroughly," he told us, "and they've removed some stuff. We're going to have to get you a new wastepaper basket for your bathroom."

"Where is Clarice, and when can we see her?" asked Susie.

"She's at Monticello Hospital. Her parents are with her, and they plan to take her home pretty soon."

"How is she?" asked Mary-Ann.

"I'm not at liberty to give you details of her injuries, but I believe she's going to be okay. She's pretty shaken up, emotionally. You know? The poor kid was laying out there in the woods."

"What about her boyfriend?"

"You didn't hear this from me, but Denny is in police custody."

"Did he do this?" asked Mary-Ann.

"Let's just say that Clarice had more than one mishap a few days ago."

"Was it those goddamn bimmies that work in the kitchen?" asked Sabra.

"Watch your mouth, Sabra," said Marsha. "You're talking to Mr. Ariti, for Christ's sake."

Ariti put up a placating hand, and said, "Everyone, please just calm down. I'm sure that Clarice will want to see you before her parents take her home. I'll bring you to the hospital myself. But I don't know if they'll let all of you in the room at the same time. You may have to go in in pairs. I've already spoken with her parents. Clarice's father is ready to shoot Denny, so it's probably best that they leave town soon."

"I knew she had no business seeing that dumbass in pink pants," said Marsha. "He was too old for her."

"Also, too married," said Ariti.

"Oh, man," said Susie. "If my guy is also married, I'm going to kill him."

"That's enough talk about killing for one day, girls. Nobody's dead yet."

"What about Rita?" asked Mary-Ann.

"I haven't heard anything from her cousin or the police on that matter," said Ariti.

"Are the police looking at both cases at once?" I asked. "Do they suspect a connection?"

"I don't know, Amy. One incident did occur very shortly after the other."

"Sounds like we've had multiple incidents," I said. "And what's the deal with the shoes? How did they get into the cabin? And how did whoever brought them in know whose bed to put them under? And is it the same person who's been taking our money all along?"

"All good questions, Amy," said Ariti. "At this moment, I don't have any answers for you. The investigation will be ongoing until it's all solved. In the meantime, the hotel is hiring an extra security guard, and not bringing in another waitress. There'll be more money for you girls. More work, too. Can you handle it?"

"We all said, "Yes."

"Can we continue to stay at the hotel?" asked Marsha.

"I'm afraid not," said Ariti. "The suite is already reserved for the rest of the summer, and we're booked solid everywhere else. But we are going to keep a closer eye on all of you. No more disappearing cocktail waitresses. We can't have the guests pouring their own wine, especially on Friday nights." He winked.

"Yeah, bring on those shiksas," said Susie.

We all huffed with laughter, including Ariti.

"Can we keep Drew as our very own security guard?" asked Sabra.

"He'll be around on occasion, but all of the guards will take their shifts, said Ariti. "Behave yourself, Sabra," he added with a smile. "Okay, girls, it's time to go to work. We've got a B'nai B'rith convention."

Marsha grimaced, and said, "Can I have the night off? I'm allergic to seltzer."

"How about I give you a great station in the cocktail lounge for next week's singles weekend?" asked Ariti.

Marsha nodded, and said, "Let's take care of those B'nai B'rith folks! Fill those peanut bowls!"

"That's the spirit," said Ariti.

# CHAPTER 13

Sabra didn't bother going to the hospital the next day. After we got back to the cabin, she decided to take advantage of our absence by having a go at Drew the security guard. She wasn't that close to Clarice, anyway. Drew probably didn't have a problem with it. Sabra had a reputation, and what did he care? She was anybody's.

Ariti picked us up in his glacier-white Buick Electra 225. Susie sat in front, and Mary-Ann, Marsha, and I took the back seat. It was plenty roomy back there. It felt like we were on the Lusitania.

We took a few back roads and were at the hospital within fifteen minutes. Ariti told us to wait while he scoped out the situation. He came back a few minutes later with visitor badges. He said, "Two at a time, ten minutes a visit."

When Marsha and I entered Clarice's room together, we saw that she was in a neck brace and propped up on two fat pillows. She turned slightly when she saw us come in and gave us a smile. I could see fading bruises on the lower part of her face.

"My God, Clarice," I said. "How are you feeling?"

"A whole lot better than a few days ago," she said. "My parents are taking me home, you know."

"Yes, we do know," said Marsha. "What in the world happened, Clarice? Can you tell us anything?"

"I can tell you that Denny is going down for roughing me up and not telling me about his wife and kids," Clarice said.

"That son of a bitch," Marsha said.

"Exactly," said Clarice.

"Well, why did Denny get rough with you?" I asked.

"We had an argument about the seriousness of our relationship," Clarice said.

"What is that supposed to mean?"

"Well, you know I haven't had much experience. He told me he loved me and, where I come from, when a guy tells you that he loves you, that usually ends in a marriage proposal. That was my expectation, but that's when Denny told me he was already married. With two kids, no less. I mean, dang."

"The word 'dang' does come to mind," I said. "But it doesn't explain why he maybe hit you."

"Oh, he definitely hit me," said Clarice. "I told him I thought I was pregnant."

"Oh, shit," said Marsha. "Are you?"

"As it turns out, I was," said Clarice. "Not anymore, though. "

"You're lucky," I said.

"I don't see it that way. He hit me really hard and damaged my girlie parts. I may never get pregnant again."

"I am so sorry, Clarice," I said. "I hope that's not true. You'll find a decent, single guy, some day. You'll have a family. I'm sure of it."

I didn't know what the hell to say.

"Well," she said. "I won't be going back to the cabin."

"I'm not too thrilled about being there myself," I said. "Ariti is arranging for around-the-clock security. I hope that Sabra allows them to concentrate, especially Drew."

"Who is Drew?" asked Clarice.

"He's one of the security guards we never knew existed," I said. "He's cute. Sabra is already all over him."

"Great. Good luck with that," said Clarice. "Whoever attacked me on the trail apparently knew where I lived. How else could my shoes have landed under my bed?"

"Are you sure you didn't put your shoes under the bed yourself?" I asked. "I mean, you were pretty messed up. Are you forgetting this one detail?"

"No, I was attacked before I ever made it to the cabin. Somebody grabbed a hold of me from the back, and I went down. I had taken the shoes off because they were squeezing my feet, but I dropped them near or on the path."

"So, nobody knows how they got under your bed?" I asked.

41

"The police are investigating that. They questioned me about it, too. They're thinking that whoever put the shoes in the cabin was the person who took our money from the bureau, but nobody knows yet."

"Very comforting," Marsha muttered.

"So, now you'll be going back to Texas," I said.

Marsha said, "We're going to miss you, Clarice. I hate that you're going home, especially like this."

"Not more than I," said Clarice. "Daddy is going to be even more protective now."

"You know, Clarice, whoever laid you down in the woods could have done more harm to you," I said. "I'm sorry you don't have any recall of what happened."

"Well, I was dead tired, and my insides were hurting. All I had on my mind was getting back to the cabin and going to sleep. I went by the kitchen with all those cretins hissing, 'Chocha, chocha,' and didn't give them any mind. Then, all of a sudden, I was grabbed from behind. I had been bleeding all night and felt weak. It's a miracle I made it through my shift. My pockets were full of cash, too. Those firemen are great tippers. All I remember is that those hands around my throat and mouth were slender. I know that because I reached up to get them away from me. But they applied a little pressure on my neck, and I went down. I don't remember much after that. Some of my injuries are from being dragged over the gravel, but most of them are from Denny in the car.

"I hope they throw the book at that bastard," Marsha said.

"He'd better hope that they keep him in custody,' said Clarice. "Daddy will kill him for sure."

"What about the wife?" I asked. "Does she know?"

"Turns out, they have a summer arrangement. She stays in White Plains with the kids, and he stays here and seduces young cocktail waitresses."

"I truly hate this guy, Clarice," I said. "Are they going to get him for assault, at least?"

"Yes, they are," said Clarice. "And, if I can get him for murder, I will. He killed my baby."

"How far along were you?" Marsha asked.

"Not very far," said Clarice. "He wanted me to get an abortion, and I wouldn't. I'm a Catholic."

"Oh, for Christ's sake," said Marsha.

I gave Marsha a look.

"I don't know what the age of viability is these days, Clarice," I said. "But he did do you grievous bodily harm, resulting in a miscarriage. And he's an asshole, to boot."

"I'm going to miss you girls," said Clarice. "I'll probably spend the rest of the summer under lock and key. I may need to come back here to testify. First, there's the Denny thing. But then, there's the matter of the secondary assault."

"Was it the bimmies?" asked Marsha.

"You know what?" said Clarice. "For all their 'chochas' and 'mamacitas,' I've never felt that threatened by them. It was always just background noise for me. Those skinny little losers with their cigarettes and white t-shirts."

Suddenly, Clarice's eyes locked with mine.

"I didn't smell cigarette smoke," she said.

"What are you saying?" I asked.

"Whoever put their hand around my mouth didn't smell of cigarettes. In fact, I smelled something sweet."

"Maybe you were just smelling baked goods from the kitchen – or something from the dumpsters," Marsha said.

"No, it was sweeter than that," said Clarice.

"Like perfume?" I asked.

"Yes," said Clarice. "Just like perfume."

# CHAPTER 14

Mark and I were spending some time in the cabin, fooling around. It was the middle of the day, and only Marsha was present. It was almost like having the cabin to ourselves. I thought we were being quiet, but every once in while Marsha would say, "Y'all sound so cute."

Mark was whispering, "I love you, and I love you, and I love you," in my ear. I was enjoying it when, suddenly, what sounded like quarter-sized hail was pelting against the window behind our heads.

"What the hell is that?" I yelled.

Mark was on top of me, so he pressed down on his arms and arched his back so he could look out the window.

"Ah, shit," he said. "It's Jean."

"Who in the world is Jean?" I asked as more gravel rained down on the glass. "And why is she throwing rocks at my window?"

The window was partly ajar, and debris was falling through the mesh screen. Mark swiftly threw back the thin blanket, jumped off of me, and put his pants on. Marsha sat on her bed pretending to read, but I could see her eyes over the top of her book, admiring Mark's muscular physique. She said, "Should I be hiding under my bed?"

"Who's Jean?" I repeated, ignoring her, as Mark went to the cabin door.

"She's an ex-girlfriend; a hostess in the dining room, ok?" he said. "Just close the window, and stay in the cabin. I'll handle this."

Mark headed out, and I could hear all sorts of abuse being thrown at him. I looked out the window, and a slim blonde threw a handful of gravel in his direction. He ducked out of the way, approached her quickly, and grabbed her wrists with both hands. The blonde struggled to break free, but she did not succeed. Mark kept on telling her to "calm down, calm down, calm down." He liked to say things in threes.

Jean was yelling, "You did it again, you son of a bitch!"

She tried to get in a few kicks, but was having trouble connecting. Mark was dancing around. He was actually a very good dancer.

"What are you talking about?" Mark yelled back. "We haven't been together in weeks!"

"And yet, I'm pregnant again!," she railed.

"What makes you think it's mine?" shouted Mark. "How many times can you get pregnant in one summer? It's not possible!"

"It's yours, three times, and it is!" she bellowed, addressing all of his objections.

"I'm not buying that it's mine this time," said Mark, "but I'll help you get rid of it again, if it'll make you happy. Just stay away from this cabin."

"Does your girlfriend know that your face should be plastered on every Planned Parenthood clinic in the country: Wanted Dead or Alive?"

"I guess she knows now. Maybe the whole damn hotel knows. How did you even know I was here?"

"Isn't this your stupid Carmen Ghia?" she asked.

She broke away and kicked one of his front tires.

"Stop kicking my car, and get the hell out of here. You and I were over in June."

Jean stalked off toward the dining staff's boardinghouse in the back forty. "You'll pay for this," she said, over her shoulder.

"I always do," Mark said to her retreating back.

—

When Mark reentered the cabin, Marsha was putting a towel into a beach bag, preparing to leave for the lake. She said, "See you later," to me and gave Mark a look on her way out.

I sat on the bed with my knees up and the sheet pulled over my chest.

"Girl trouble?" I asked.

"You could say that," said Mark.

"I knew you were the knock-up king of the Catskills, but three times in one summer?" I said. "And all with the same woman? Are there more?"

45

"No, there are no more," said Mark.

He sat on the edge of my bed and looked at me.

"I swear, Amy, you're the only woman I've been with since June. I don't know if Jean is pregnant by me or not, but I will handle it. I meant what I said to you. I love you and you alone."

I loved Mark, too, but there was no shortage of eligible young men at Hoffman's. It wasn't like I was dying to be with someone else. I just didn't want to have to deal with Mark's crazed ex. I was having enough trouble with that miserable foreman, Julius, taunting me while I worked the main dining room. I didn't need a jealous hostess tripping me up. And yet, breaking up with Mark didn't appeal to me.

"What should we do?" I asked. "Should we take a break?"

"What, and let you meet someone else? Hell, no, we don't take a break," he said, reaching for me. "You don't worry about Jean. You let *me* worry about Jean."

"I don't know, Mark. Women are dropping like flies around here."

"Nothing's going to happen to you. I can promise you that."

How could anybody ever promise that to anyone? This was shaping up to be a hell of a summer. And it was only mid-July. Anything could happen to anyone. But I was nineteen. I looked into Mark's green eyes and saw nothing but adoration there.

I said, "Have you noticed we're alone in the cabin, for a change?"

"That hasn't escaped my notice," he said.

He took off his pants and slipped back into the bed beside me.

# CHAPTER 15

Rita put on a kimono and wrapped her short, wet hair in a towel. Sitting on the edge of the bed, she flicked her Bic and lit a Benson and Hedges. Taking a deep drag, she settled back against the pillow, crossing her long legs at the ankle. She released a plume of smoke into the patterned ceiling tiles. It had been an exhausting couple of weeks. She closed her eyes and anticipated a knock on the door.

It came.

"Room service," announced a male voice.

Rita snuffed out her cigarette in the ashtray on the nightstand.

"Just a minute," she said.

She slipped her legs off the bed and put on a pair of red stilettos. Undoing the sash on her robe, Rita strode over to the door. At the last minute, she remembered the towel on her head and tossed it onto a nearby chair. She ran a hand through her hair and opened the door. When she saw who was standing there, she quickly backed up, hastily retying her sash. It was actually the room service guy with a bottle of champagne in a chilled bucket with two long-stemmed flutes and bud vase with a single white rose.

"I hope I'm not disturbing you, ma'am," said the server.

Rita collected herself, and said, "Not at all. I was just expecting somebody else."

"Do I have the wrong room?" asked the server. He frowned down at his order pad.

"I don't know, said Rita. "I wasn't expecting room service."

The server said, "Room 312, Rita Connelly, right?"

"That's correct."

"Where would you like me to put this, ma'am?"

Rita looked around, and said, "How about on that table by the window?"

While the server was busy setting out his order, Rita went into the closet and removed a five-dollar bill from her purse. She approached the server, and asked, "Can you tell me who sent this?"

"There's a card propped up against the vase," he said. "Will that be all, ma'am?"

"Yes, thank you," she said, handing him the five. He accepted the bill, and left with the cart. She latched the door behind him.

Rita approached the small, pink envelope like it was a coiled snake. The guy she was expecting wasn't one to make romantic gestures. He was one to wonder where the champagne came from. As she reached out for the envelope, she was interrupted by another knock on the door. She was going to have to think fast. She snatched up the card and buried it in her pocket.

"Who is it?" she sang out.

"It's me. Open up already. Whaddya doing in there?"

"I'm coming, honey, give me a sec."

Rita caught a view of herself in the mirror and noticed that she was sweating. She was going to have to take another shower, but there was no time now.

Leaving her sash tied this time, Rita took a deep breath and unlocked the door. She immediately brought him in and wrapped her right leg around him, pulling him close. He kissed her on the mouth and abruptly disengaged.

"It's hot as hell in here," he said, stalking over to the thermostat and jacking it down low.

"I just got out of a shower," said Rita. "I didn't want to catch a chill."

"You're still wet, baby," he said, getting more interested in her sash. He used it to reel her toward him. Rita fell into his arms. He back-walked her toward the bed and gave her a gentle push. She dropped onto the soft mattress, and he got on top of her. She wanted to keep him there as long as possible. She needed time to think. Her spiky heels dented the flowered bedspread as he sank inside of her.

"Rocco," she breathed.

They moved together like a couple in love. When they were finished, Rocco got up to light a cigarette and went to look out the window.

48

"What's with *this* stuff?" he asked, noticing the champagne and rose on the table.

"Well, we're celebrating, aren't we?" said Rita.

"I don't know," he asked. "What are we celebrating?"

"The end of my job," said Rita. "Mission accomplished, right?"

"Yeah, baby, you done good," said Rocco. "But now, there's another job."

"You told me two weeks, tops."

"Yeah. Two weeks per job."

"I didn't sign up for that," said Rita.

Rocco reached for the champagne bottle and popped the cork.

"Come on, baby. Let's celebrate our partnership. We have a good thing going here."

Rita said, "I don't like ripping people off, Rocco. Come on. I've paid my debt."

"One more time and that's it, I promise. One more time for you and the kid."

—

Rita was living with her cousin and his wife and their disabled son in Ellenville, New York, when she met Rocco in a restaurant one night. She was waiting tables, and he was sitting alone at the bar, watching her. He was strikingly handsome with his olive skin, pale gray eyes, and prematurely silver hair. It was a quiet night, so she went over to say, "Hello."

He told her he was a businessman, and she told him she was doing whatever she could to help her cousin care for his sick child. Rita had recently divorced. Her husband had left her with nothing other than what she was able to take and hide from him.

Rocco had asked Rita if she was interested in making a few extra bucks.

"I won't have to sell myself, will I?" she joked.

"Nah," he said. "Nothing like that. Think of it as an acting job."

"What?" she laughed, "I don't know how to act."

49

"All you'll need to do is wait tables, just like now," he said. "You'll also have to cut your hair pretty short."

Rita touched her upswept dark hair, as if making sure it was still there. "I like my hair long," she said. "Why would I have to cut it?"

"Because you're going to have to wear a wig," said Rocco. "I told ya, it's an acting job. A wig is part of the costume."

"What part am I playing?" asked Rita.

"A part that you're perfect for; a cocktail waitress at one of those big Catskill hotels. Those girls make great money doing that."

"You want to get me a job as a cocktail waitress at a Catskill resort? I already have a job."

"You can't be making squat working in a place like this."

"I can't argue with that," said Rita. "Do you have contacts? I mean, don't you need to know someone to get a job in one of those resorts?"

"I know people," he said. "I know a guy named George Ariti at Hoffman's. He'll take you in, no questions asked.

"Why wouldn't he ask any questions?" she asked. "And why all the cloak and dagger?"

"You ask a lot of questions for a waitress, you know?"

"I need to know what I'm getting myself into."

"Hey, George Ariti isn't the only guy I know. I know your ex, all right?"

"You know Marty? Does Marty have something to do with this?"

"Yeah," said Rocco. "He told me you weren't above stealing."

"I was desperate," said Rita.

"I'm guessing you still are," said Rocco.

"I'm getting by," she said, turning to walk away.

Rocco took her by the arm.

"If you aren't above stealing, I want you to do a little job for me. Two week, tops."

"What if I say, 'No'?" Rita asked.

"Then, I'm afraid I'll have to kill you. I just incriminated myself, didn't I?"

Rocco smiled like a malevolent crocodile. Rita gave him a long look, and said, "I can't abandon my nephew. Whatever I do, my family life

50

remains unchanged, and you stay away from them. I know the owners here. I'll tell them I need a couple of weeks off."

"Do what you gotta do," said Rocco. "Just don't get too close to anyone at the resort. Do your job, earn your pay, and bring me the rest. You'll figure out how. And you'll show up for breakfast at your cousin's place the next morning."

"How am I supposed to go back and forth? I don't have a car."

We'll work it out," said Rocco. "I'll find a way to get you back and forth to Center Street."

Rita said, "You know where I live? How long have you been following me around? What else do you know about me?"

Rocco said, "I know all about you, Rita."

# CHAPTER 16

Rita stood waiting at the intersection of Center Street and North Main Street. Rocco told her to expect a light blue Ford Pinto to pick her up at 3 p.m. It was her first day of work at Hoffman's. She was told to arrive an hour early for orientation and to pick up her uniforms. She was instructed to bring her own red and blue high heels. Rocco said he would pick up the cost of the shoes.

That day, Rita carried both pairs of shoes in a paper sack, along with a few other items she thought she might need. When the Pinto pulled up, she walked tentatively to the curb and looked in. The man sitting inside gestured for her to hurry up. Rita opened the door.

"You Rita?" asked the man.

Rita nodded.

"Get in," he said. "It's a half-hour to Hoffman's. You don't want to be late on your first day."

Rita slid into the passenger seat and placed her bag between her feet. She glanced at the driver out of the corner of her eye, but otherwise kept her gaze forward. The man took off as soon as she closed the car door.

"Here's the deal," said the man. "I pick you up every afternoon for the next couple of weeks at the same intersection. After today, I'll be picking you up at 4. You'll have a bed there, but you won't be sleeping in it. Another car will be picking you up after work. It'll be a red Mustang."

"What's your name?" asked Rita.

"You don't need to know," he said. "But if you want to call me something, I'm Joe."

Rita said, "Okay, Joe."

Joe said, "Now I want you to look in the back seat. There's a box back there. I want you to get that box, and open it up."

"What is it?" Rita asked.

"Just open it up, and do what I tell you."

Rita leaned over the back seat and hefted the box. It felt solid, but not too heavy. She placed it on her lap and opened the lid. There was wig inside on a stand. If Rocco hadn't said anything about a wig beforehand, she might have thought it was a severed head. It was on the short side, dark blonde, and wavy.

"Put it on," said Joe.

Rita had never worn a wig before. She detached it from the stand and placed it on her head. It was lopsided, and she tried to adjust it.

"Your hair's too long," said Joe. "Weren't you told to cut it?"

"I didn't get a chance," lied Rita. "I'll make it work. But how's it supposed to stay on? Are there clips or something?"

"How the hell do I know?" asked Joe. "Do I look like a guy who knows how to wear a wig?" He pointed to his own shaggy brown hair. "I think it clips to the back of your head, or something."

Rita felt around and found a fastener. She attached the wig to her hair and swept the rest of her tresses beneath it. She opened her purse and withdrew a compact. Looking in the tiny mirror, she made some adjustments. She applied more lipstick while she was at it. When she was satisfied, she turned to Joe, and said, "What do you think?"

Joe briefly turned his eyes from the road, and said, "Not bad."

Rita noted that Joe was about her age. He had a pleasant face, and his hands looked large on the steering wheel.

Rita turned back to face forward and sat in nervous anticipation. Traffic was light that day. It wasn't long before they were turning in to Hoffman's. The sign in front said, "Leave Your Troubles at the Gate!"

"Today," said Joe, "I'm going to drive you all the way up to the main house. Tomorrow, I'll be dropping you by the path that leads to your room. They've got you in a cabin with some other women."

"Okay," said Rita.

"When you get into the main house, ask to speak with George Ariti. He's the boss of the cocktail waitresses."

"I've heard that name before," said Rita.

"Yeah?" said Joe. "I hear he's a good guy. He'll get you situated in your room. Well, maybe not him personally, but someone will show you where you'll be staying. Only you won't be staying."

53

"Won't the other waitresses wonder about that?"

"Tell them you've got a boyfriend. Or make something up. They don't need to know your whole life story. And you said you don't want to get your family involved. We respect that. You're there to do your job and make money, just like everyone else. Don't get too cozy with anybody."

"Okay."

"You got any questions?"

"No, I know what I'm here to do," said Rita. "What choice do I have?"

"Marty's not interested in giving you any choices, Rita. Remember, the Mustang will be here to pick you up at 4 a.m.

Rita took her bag and got out of the car without looking back.

# CHAPTER 17

T he girls and I first met Rita on the job. She started about an hour after we did and was given a relatively quiet station. I guess that Ariti wanted to see how she did before he sent her into the lion's den. Turns out, she was a very good waitress: fast, friendly, and accurate. Unlike me, she didn't have any accidents. She handled the little tray and stilettos with ease. She clearly had experience, and, at twice our ages, a lot more than we had.

Rita was nice enough to us, but she obviously didn't want to talk about herself. I remember her hovering over her cot, laying out pieces of her uniform, and putting everything on with care. She wore a little watch on her left wrist, and a locket around her neck. If there were pictures in there, she never showed them to us.

We didn't get the wig at all, but figured it was none of our business if she wanted to wear one. It was the early 1970s. Women, and some men, were wearing wigs just for the fun of it. But most of those wigs were just plain goofy, like big hair in psychedelic colors. Rita's wig was very conservative-looking, like she was somebody's mother on the way to a luncheon. She also wore glasses around her neck on a chain. She used them when she was ringing up somebody's bill.

We never saw Rita come or go. She just appeared and disappeared like magic. She was always a little late and always left a little early because there was somewhere else she needed to be in the middle of the night. She did tell us she had a boyfriend named Rocco, and we assumed she was connecting with him. But we weren't sure.

Ariti seemed to be okay with her erratic schedule. I'm not sure he knew whether she was sleeping in the cabin or not. Business was pretty slow before 5 p.m. and after 3 a.m. anyway. We were happy to fill in for her when she wasn't there. More money for us.

If this was intended to be a temporary gig for Rita, she never let us know that. She just kept on showing up on the job every night. She did use the cabin to change into her uniform. We assumed that she returned to the cabin to change before leaving to points unknown after work because she took her belongings with her, including both pairs of shoes. If she were coming back the next day, I don't know why she bothered dragging all that stuff around. Maybe she overheard us talking about the money that was going missing, but, so far, no one was running off with our shoes or clothing.

It was upsetting when our tips disappeared, and we suspected Rita. But none of us felt comfortable accusing her directly, and it wasn't happening every night. She never put her own money in the drawer. We assumed she just took her earnings with her when she went to wherever she went every night. After a while, we just hid our money elsewhere and put it in the bank every chance we got. Only Marsha kept forgetting and continued to put her tips in the drawer. Sleep deprivation and twelve-hour shifts addled her.

We wondered if Rita had a family somewhere. She never mentioned anyone, outside of Rocco, and we never asked. I mean, she was a full-grown woman, and she really didn't feel like one of us. We were curious about her, but not enough to probe. We were young women involved with boyfriends. We served drinks at night while performers like Jackie Mason and Totie Fields did their routines on stage. We ate on the run, slept little, had sex at every opportunity, lounged at the lake, and went back to work.

Hoffman's wasn't a career for us. It was a summer job while we attended colleges all over the country. Labor Day was it for us. After that, we packed up our few possessions and headed back home, usually in our fathers' cars. We had no other means of transportation. We would spend a couple of weeks with our families in Richmond or Binghamton and then get carted off to school. That's the way it worked for all of us, but not Rita.

We considered Rita a townie and probably a career waitress. We just didn't know which town she was from. There were plenty of them in the Catskills; places like Ferndale and Ellenville and South Fallsburg and Bethel, which is where Woodstock had taken place a few years before. In fact, the camp I had worked at was right next to Max Yasgur's farm.

56

How did Rita end up at Hoffman's with a bunch of college kids? It was a puzzlement, but we didn't give it that much thought until she left and didn't come back. Marsha wanted to go through the shopping bag she left behind, I guess to see if she would find our missing cash there. I didn't feel right going through her belongings, especially because she was such a private person and all. But Marsha insisted. She sifted through the sack and just found the two uniforms, neatly folded, the two pairs of pumps, a change of underwear, and a makeup bag. No money.

Had she been more thorough, Marsha might have discovered the powdery white residue on the bottom of the sack.

So, we just delivered the bag to Ariti, and he told us he would keep it in the safe in his office until Rita showed up to retrieve it, or until someone else arrived making inquiries. That's when Lovato appeared and left with a bag laced with heroin.

# CHAPTER 18

Rita didn't have that big of a role to play. All she needed to do was slip a few bags of horse to Drew the security guard, for which she would receive a pre-calculated sum of money in an envelope. It was a simple exchange, and Rita would get a five percent cut, which would be paid out to her when she finished the job. She never asked where the heroin came from or whose nose it ended up in. Her transactions with Drew were both secret and silent. She once brought the subject up with Joe, her usual driver, but he shook his head at her, and she didn't ask twice.

Rita didn't like being a drug mule, but she figured that the whole sordid affair was going to be over with within a couple of weeks; that she'd pay off her ex and move on. She didn't know where her relationship with Rocco was headed. When she agreed to working with him, she knew she was lying down with the devil. But she had been drawn to him from the get-go. She had a history of being attracted to the wrong men, which is what got her into this fix to begin with. She knew it with every fiber of her being, and yet, she gave in.

In the meantime, she was seeing her family less and less. She did send money to her mother in New Jersey, but they didn't speak much. Her mother had her own problems, and, for most of her young life, Rita had been one of them. Rita had run with a rough crowd. She figured that it was better to leave her mother in peace and make restitution to the best of her ability for the trials she had put her through. She was better off in her cousin's house, for now. She felt safe there and, while she helped with groceries and her sick nephew, her room over the garage was rent-free.

When Rocco came along, she found herself spending more and more time with him. She had no idea where he lived, even though she had met him in her cousin's town, Ellenville. They always met at a hotel, a different one each time, and in different towns in the area. They never went out together; just ordered room service. She was always registered as Rita Connelly. Her last name was still Gold, her married name, but was previously Lovato, like her cousin's. She needed to change that, but she hadn't gotten around to it. And Rocco never wanted to see her with her wig on. It was exclusively for work at Hoffman's. He still got on her case for not cutting her hair.

"What's the big deal?" she asked. "I'm wearing the wig at work, like you asked me to."

"Your hair's too big for that wig," he said.

"I'll be done in a few days," she said. "I'm managing."

He never told her he had bigger plans for her. Eventually, he told her he just loved short hair. That's when she decided she would cut it, to surprise him at the end of the gig.

Rita wondered what Rocco did for a living, if he was married, if he had children. She found herself falling for him, despite the dangerous position he had put her in. She hated herself for being a patsy and wondered how she could be so stupid.

Her life with Marty had started out fine and ended up badly. She had met him ten years before, shortly after she had been released from the women's prison in Ossining, New York. She hadn't been there long. She had served a little time for breaking and entering with intent to commit burglary. As a teenager, she had gotten into trouble for forging checks and shoplifting. But, with maturity, Rita had straightened herself out. She got work as a waitress and moved into her own small apartment in Elmira, New York.

Rita had met Marty Gold through a couple she had gotten friendly with on the job. Marty was a successful stockbroker and recent widower. Her friends didn't know anything about her former life aside from growing up a child of divorce in Hoboken, New Jersey. Rita didn't lack in the looks department, and had an independent streak that some men found attractive. Marty and Rita began to date, and he became smitten with her. His young wife had died in the passenger seat of a car he was driving, the victim of a hit and run. There were no children.

A couple of years had passed since the accident, and Marty was lonely. He had dated plenty of women since the loss of his wife, but Rita was the only one who had intrigued him with her grit and mysteriousness. He sensed she was hiding something, and he tried to solve the puzzle. But

Rita didn't want him to know that she had spent time in prison. She just wanted a safe home with a man who wouldn't probe too deeply. She wasn't in love with him, but he was okay, and she agreed to marry him. She didn't expect it to last forever. Nobody was more of a transient than Rita.

Marty wasn't interested in having a working wife. Besides, it wasn't appropriate for a broker to have a wife waiting tables at the local steakhouse. For the first time in her life, Rita didn't have to worry about where her next dime was coming from. Marty took care of all her material needs. It was the middle 1960s. All Marty asked of Rita was to prepare his meals, wear the skimpy lingerie he bought for her, and iron his shirts while he watched porn. She didn't even need to clean up. Marty got her a housekeeper. It was easy street.

And then the subject of kids came up. It all went downhill from there.

# CHAPTER 19

The summer was winding down. I was still with Mark, and we were happy together. His ex-girlfriend, Jean, stopped throwing rocks at my window, although she did shoot me a dirty look in the dining room once in a while. Good thing I mostly worked in the nightclub and cocktail lounge. Jean still liked me better than Julius did. I was able to avoid her, but Julius followed me around the dining room making insulting remarks until I called him a nasty little worm one day. Then, he stopped talking to me altogether, which made my dining room gig much easier. Sometimes, you've just got to speak up.

Susie was still seeing her boyfriend, Jack, the health club manager. Like Clarice's Denny, he was also an old guy, but at least he wasn't married, as far as we knew. Susie wasn't as innocent as she was at the beginning of the summer, but she hadn't completely sold her soul to the devil. Jack treated her with respect and affection, and he was pleasant with all of us, so no big trouble there.

Susie was the one who was keeping in the most touch with Clarice, who was stuck at home with her parents and younger siblings in Dallas. Denny had pleaded guilty to aggravated assault charges with hopes of receiving a lighter sentence. He was no longer working at Hoffman's, and we heard that his wife had filed for divorce. At some point, Clarice was going to have to return to New York to deal with the other assault, the one that had left her bleeding and unconscious in the woods.

Mary-Ann was still hanging out with Louis, the maître de. He was very rough with her, but she didn't seem to mind it. None of the rest of us wanted him to spend any time in the cabin, and we expressed ourselves to Mary-Ann, who told us she understood. She took to spending more time at his place.

Marsha's Johnny had gone to work elsewhere. I'm still not sure what he was doing at Hoffman's, unless it was a little bit of this and a little bit of that. So, Marsha had connected with another guy, named Max, who

61

was a waiter in the guest dining room. When he wasn't serving kreplach, he was a pre-med student at Dartmouth. Marsha had definitely traded up, and we all liked him.

And Sabra was Sabra. She continued to use her body to make money on the side and had a big thing going on with Drew the security guard. Every time we entered the cabin, there they were on Sabra's skinny cot in the corner. We were seeing Drew entirely too much and starting to resent the extra loss of privacy. It was bad enough that we were all living right on top of each other without having his firearms and other security guard crap lying around, usually on top of our beds. Plus, he was supposed to be protecting all of us, not just the one he was screwing on the job.

Marsha threatened to report Drew to his boss, Mike. After all, Drew wasn't there just to protect us from a petty thief. Two women had gone missing from the cabin, and one had been found pretty banged up. The other one could be dead, altogether. We didn't know, and we were all nervous about the situation.

I didn't worry much when I was with Mark because he was strong as an ox and he looked like a street fighter. Jack was also not a lightweight in the strength department. Louis and Max were a little soft. I didn't see them duking it out with anyone, except maybe each other. Max was very nice, but nobody liked Louis, including Max. He wondered why Mary-Ann allowed him to push her around, but he minded his own business.

None of us, except maybe Drew, was equipped to apprehend a killer, if one should show up. And we didn't know how effective Drew would be if someone broke in while he was doing the hokey pokey with Sabra. We were probably better off that Charlie worked at night, when most of the bad stuff had gone down. Drew was almost always assigned the day shift.

"I'm glad the summer's almost over," said Marsha, one day. "I don't know how much more of this I can take."

"Just another month, or so, until Labor Day," I said. "Then, we can clear out and go back to school."

"Yeah," Marsha said, "If we're still alive."

"I wonder if Clarice will return while we're still here," I said.

"I doubt she would want to return to the scene of the crime," said Marsha. "I think she'll more likely be sitting in a deposition room somewhere. I don't really know how all that works, outside of old 'Perry Mason' shows. I think that they have to formally interrogate her, or something; have her go over, once more, what happened to her, and why. That's probably going to be pretty humiliating. I wonder if they'll send her parents out of the room. Can you imagine having to discuss any of that stuff in front of your mother and father? That would just kill me."

"Well, she almost *actually* got killed," I said. "*Twice.*"

"True," said Marsha.

"What is her father, some kind of cowboy?" I asked.

"I think Clarice told me he's an insurance salesman."

"Oh, I said. "Forgive the stereotype. I guess my father, the dermatologist, would be pretty murderous, too, if *I* got assaulted. *Twice.*"

"Oh, my daddy would go berserk," Marsha said.

"Anyway, we have a few weeks to get through this summer in one piece," I said. "Are you planning to continue to see Max?"

"Oh, I sure hope so. Of course, he'll be up in New Hampshire, and I'll be down in Virginia, but I'm sure we'll try to see each other. What about you and Mark?"

"Oh, I think we'll continue to see each other, at least for a while," I said. "I think *I'm* pregnant."

# CHAPTER 20

oly shit," said Marsha. "Are you serious?"

"Well," I said, "with me, you never know. I'm pretty irregular, so a late period doesn't have to be anything to get hysterical about."

"Are you feeling sick?"

"Not particularly, but my boobs hurt more than usual."

"Are you going to get a test?"

"I think I'd better. I'm nineteen and have years of schooling left. I'm not ready to be a mother."

"Have you spoken to Mark yet?"

"Nope. You're the first person I've spoken to about this."

We were interrupted by a knock on the door. I was expecting Mark and had heard his Carmen Ghia crunching to a halt outside the cabin seconds before. I told Marsha I would have more to talk about later and opened the door. Mark took me in his arms and kissed me.

"Ready to go?" he asked.

"Yes, let me just grab a sweater," I said, disappearing into the closet.

"Hi, Marsha," said Mark, noticing her for the first time.

Marsha gazed at Mark for a few seconds before responding.

"Hi, Mark," she finally said.

I popped out of the closet and looped my arm through Mark's. "Vamanos, muchacho," I said, cheerfully.

We were going to take a ride in the country, at my suggestion. We had something to talk about. I hoped our conversation was going to go better than the one Clarice had had with Denny. We said, "Bye," to Marsha and headed out.

As we motored down the highway, I suggested that we pull into a scenic overlook. Mark was happy to do so. He pulled into a parking space and turned the car off. He turned to look at me and put his hands on the sides of my face. I saw pure adoration in his eyes and wondered if that look would change once I expressed myself. It wasn't exactly news yet. I didn't know whether I was pregnant or not.

I smiled at him lovingly because that was how I felt, and said, "I have to say something to you."

I saw his eyes narrow slightly.

"Are you all right?" he asked.

"Oh, yes, I'm just fine," I said.

Not wanting to be suspenseful, I said, "I'm late, Mark."

A happy smile bloomed on his face.

"That's fantastic!" he said, kissing me exuberantly on the lips. "I couldn't be more thrilled! Let's get married!"

"I don't know if I'm actually pregnant or not. Let's not jump to conclusions."

"I don't care if you're pregnant or not. I want to marry you. I love you with all my heart! Let's get married and have a baby."

This is where I had to tread lightly.

"I love you, too, Mark, but I don't think I'm ready for all that. I'm only going into my sophomore year of college. I have a career to think about."

"Let me worry about a career."

"I'm sorry, babe," I said. "It can't be that way with me. I definitely need to finish my education before I can think about getting married and raising a family. Why don't I at least get a test and see if I'm actually pregnant?"

Mark's face fell toward his chest.

"Please understand," I said. "I'm not ruling out marriage forever. I'm just too young right now, is all. You have several years up on me and are already in graduate school. Let's take this one step at a time."

I turned his face to look at me, and said, "Okay?" I pulled him close and kissed him. "We'll work something out."

Mark said, "This is what we're going to do. I have a few home pregnancy tests. I picked them up in Canada the last time I was there. I guess you understand why I keep some on hand."

I huffed, "If I wasn't in this mess, I would laugh out loud."

Mark continued, "You are going to take one of those tests, and, if it's positive, you can figure out what you want to do. At the very least, you're going to need to see a doctor. If you decide you want to end the pregnancy, you're going to take a three-day leave and come home to Flatbush with me."

"But the summer's almost over," I protested.

"Shhh," he said. "If you're actually pregnant and not ready to have a baby, we will have to work fast. Trust me, I know how these things work."

I smiled, "I guess that you of all people would know."

He said, "Very funny, but yes, I do know. And, if you are pregnant and want to terminate the pregnancy, I know where you can get a safe abortion. So, you'll let me take you home for a few days. You can meet my parents, and we'll go to a place in New York that I'm familiar with to get you checked out."

I considered his proposal for a moment, and said, "Okay, I think I can get away for a few days. The other girls can share my tables. I'll just tell Ariti that I have a personal matter to attend to."

"There you go," said Mark. "But my offer is for real, Amy. I would love to have you as my wife and the mother of my children. Maybe give it some thought?"

"Maybe someday," I said. I gave him a smile. "But if you're looking for a woman who will give you a passel of children, that just isn't me. It'll be a miracle if I have one. If you or your parents have some kind of big-family plans, they're not going to like me very much."

"My parents are going to love you," said Mark, excited again. "They only had two kids themselves, and they're not looking for me to have more than that."

He started up the car as if we were heading off to Brooklyn that minute. We held hands as we sped down the highway toward no place in particular. I looked out the window at the passing rural landscapes; the rolling hills and the chicken farms; the billboards advertising hotels and bungalow colonies. The Catskills was a place for happy families.

I had always been ambivalent about having children considering I didn't have the happiest childhood myself. I wondered if I would pass along a legacy of sadness to my own offspring. My pain was so deep, I wondered if it would act as a shield against pregnancy, as if my body would just reject all possibility. On the other hand, if my body was, indeed, capable of producing life, maybe having a child of my own would somehow heal me. But that wouldn't be fair to a baby, would it?

I closed my eyes and put a hand on my belly, turning my vision inward. Mark was surely the fertility god of the Borscht Belt, and probably of the entire borough of Brooklyn, but I doubted that I was the fertility goddess of anywhere. Was I pregnant with Mark's baby? A wave of nausea swept through me as we drifted through the countryside on that late July afternoon.

# CHAPTER 21

Mark retrieved one of the pregnancy tests from his room in the boardinghouse and drove me back to my cabin which was, thankfully, empty. He called instructions through the closed bathroom door as I performed the test. I came out when I was finished, and we sat on my bed together, awaiting the result. The result was pale, but still positive. I was going to have to go to Brooklyn. I would tell Ariti that night.

Mark's parents lived on the first floor of a garden apartment in Flatbush. His mother was a petite woman with nylon stockings rolled up to her knees, and his father was a short, muscular man with all of his hair, a mustache, and suspenders. They both treated me with much warmth, and I liked them very much. In addition to Mark, they had another son who was working on a doctorate in Romanian at Harvard. I didn't know you could get a doctorate in that. Nevertheless, I had a grandfather from Bucharest, so there was a connection there.

I doubt that Mark told his parents about the pregnancy. On the day that we headed to Planned Parenthood, they thought we were going to the Metropolitan Museum of Art. There was no need to get them riled up, especially when we didn't know what was happening with me.

Shortly after I made out some paperwork and provided a urine sample, I was sent into a waiting room populated by women of all ages who were complaining about all the miseries of early pregnancy – the morning sickness, the exhaustion, the mood swings, the food cravings, and so on. I had none of those symptoms, so I just kept my mouth shut and listened to them commiserate with each other. Suddenly, a young woman in a nurse's uniform called my name, and I was asked to follow her into what I presumed would be an examining room.

She told me, "We tested your sample, and it was negative. What makes you think you're pregnant?"

"My period's late, my boobs hurt, I got a positive pregnancy test, and my boyfriend's very fertile."

"Well, those are all indicators, but it sounds like you got a false-positive. Rare, but it happens. The doctor will want to examine you."

"OK," I said.

What else was I going to say?

A doctor came in and, after a brief internal exam, he told me my uterus was barely the size of a pea and that there was no way I was pregnant. He had me provide another sample just to be sure, and the test was conclusively negative.

"I guess you dodged a bullet," said the doctor. He recommended a follow-up appointment with a regular gynecologist who would fit me for a diaphragm or IUD. "Maybe have your boyfriend wear a condom, too. He sounds like a breeder."

I thanked the doctor and nurse and left the examining room feeling greatly relieved. In fact, I felt like hugging them both.

The women in the waiting room watched me walking out with a big smile on my face. They were all there for abortions, and I was leaving scot free. I got a few dirty looks. On the other hand, I was wondering what the hell was wrong with my uterus.

Mark greeted the news with mixed emotions.

"Well, that's great," he said. "But I have to admit, I'm feeling a little disappointed."

I comforted him.

"If we were just going to terminate the pregnancy anyway, it's better that I didn't have to go through an uncomfortable procedure."

"That's true," he said.

"Plenty of time for all that later," I said.

"I guess so," he said.

But something told me that I had gotten lucky; that when the summer ended, we would likely part ways. Mark might have denied it, but I thought he was a guy who wanted lots of kids and a stay-at-home mom for a wife. I was career-bound and didn't want to end up as a housewife in a garden apartment in Flatbush, not that there was anything wrong with that. It just wasn't going to be my path. I knew it, and I think he knew it, too.

So, we said our loving good-byes to his parents and headed back to Hoffman's on a humid afternoon. Neither of us expected to work that night, so we celebrated with dinner out at a Chinese restaurant in Monticello. While we waited for a table, we saw a copy of *The New York Times* lying on a counter. The first page was face-up. The headline shouted, "GANGLAND KILLER GETS LIFE TERM: Alleged Gambino Gunman Sentenced in Monticello."

"Holy shit, will you look at this?" said Mark, picking the paper up to read the rest of the story. I didn't interrupt him. When he was finished, he handed me the paper, and I read it for myself. Mark said, "We're right in the heart of the action, baby! This is today's news!"

My eyes brushed the article, and I said, "Well, I'm glad they put the killer away, but I'm sure there's more where he comes from around here."

Mark nodded, and said, "You got that right. Weren't you up here last year when the shooting happened on 17?"

"Yes. I was a camp counselor in Bethel. Even tucked away playing color war games, we still heard about it. We just didn't pay that much attention to it. We were so sheltered."

"Well, you're not so sheltered anymore. It's a big, dangerous world out there, Amy."

"Don't I know it. I'm living in the middle of a crime scene," I said.

But at least I'm not pregnant, I thought to myself.

"Hey, how about a movie?" asked Mark.

We hadn't actually been out on a real date all summer, so I said, "Sure! I wonder what's playing here."

Mark stopped a waiter, and inquired.

"Go see *Mean Streets*," the waiter said. "Very good picture."

# CHAPTER 22

We got back pretty late that night. Mark wanted to stay over, but I needed every bit of my single bed. I was pretty worn out from my few days of "personal business." Charlie was posted on the porch when Mark walked me to the door.

"Turn away, Charlie," said Mark. "I'm going to kiss my girlfriend good night."

Charlie kindly obliged, and Mark kissed me slow and deep.

"I'll see you tomorrow," he said. "I love you, and I love you, and I love you. Don't forget it."

"I love you, too," I said. "See you tomorrow."

"Count on it," he said.

He turned and walked down the few steps to his car. He blew me a kiss as he headed toward the boardinghouse in the back forty.

I asked Charlie what I'd missed.

He said, "Did you hear they sent that Mob killer away for life?"

I said, "Yeah, I did hear. Good riddance."

He nodded, and said, "There's always more of those wise guys, you know."

"Yeah, I know," I said.

I had grown up in a neighborhood on Long Island chock full of Mafiosi, so I did know a little something. Plus, I had just seen *Mean Streets* in Monticello with Mark.

"Pretty quiet around here, though," he said. "The girls won't be done for hours. If you want to get some sleep without getting interrogated about your time off, you'd best head in now and hit the sheets. I'll be out here protecting you from the Big Bad Wolf."

"Thanks, Charlie," I said. "I really appreciate it. Any word on the incidents here?"

"Well, one word, yeah: Heroin. The authorities think that heroin's involved, at least in Rita's case."

"Why is that?"

"Well, the cops paid her cousin a visit. He had Rita's bag, you know. Still had her uniforms in there. But when they dug a little deeper, they found the white stuff."

Charlie made like he was shooting up.

"Why am I not surprised to hear this?" I said.

"People lay down with the wrong people, bad stuff happens," said Charlie. "Mark my words."

"Is there any news on Rita, aside from the heroin?" I asked, briefly alert.

"Not yet," said Charlie. "Try to get a little sleep. You look all in."

I said, "Good night," and entered the cabin. It was just as I had left it. My bed was still neatly made and I put my overnight bag on it. There wasn't much in there. I had only been away a couple of nights, but it felt like I had been away for a month. Between the pregnancy scare, the marriage proposal, the visit to Planned Parenthood, meeting Mark's parents, and the whole pea-sized uterus thing, too much had been crammed into too little time. I began to look forward to the relative quiet of another school year in a different state. I quickly unpacked, put on a nightgown, washed up, and pulled back the blanket.

There was a note there.

"Welcome back," it started. "So much to talk about," it continued. It was signed, "Marsha."

I guessed that Marsha wanted to talk about the heroin in Rita's bag and the Mafia crackdown in the area. If Charlie spoke about it to me, surely the others were aware of what was going on. Or maybe something else happened that Charlie didn't even know about. Marsha was very tuned in, and I felt confident that she would share her thoughts with me before she shared them with anyone else. We had a bond going on.

I must have been dead to the world when my roommates returned after work because, the next thing I knew, it was morning, and they were all there, sleeping in their cots, alone for a change. I was glad that none of them had disturbed me because I needed the sleep. I got up to get ready for breakfast in the staff dining room. I was looking forward to hearing Leo going through his usual routine. Maybe I would order the sauerkraut juice, for once.

Marsha opened one eye just as I was about to leave the cabin. She beckoned to me.

I walked over, and said, "I didn't want to wake you up."

"I'm glad to see you," said Marsha. "Give me a few minutes. I'll go to breakfast with you."

I said, "Okay."

Marsha pushed back the covers and swung her feet onto the linoleum floor. She removed a bag of toiletries from beneath her bed, grabbed some clothing out of the bureau, and made her way toward the bathroom. She whispered, "I'll shower later. We've got lots to talk about. But first, are you pregnant?

"No, I'm not."

Marsha wiped her forehead like a sigh of relief.

"Give me a sec," she said.

"Okay," I said again. I sat on my bed and waited.

Marsha came out of the bathroom and disappeared into the closet for a moment.

"Let's go," she said, coming out dressed.

"Give me a hint," I said, as we left the cabin.

"I think that Rita is dead," she said. "And I think that Rocco is dead, too."

# CHAPTER 23

I linked my arm through Marsha's as we headed toward the staff dining room. We passed the bimmies, who rang out the usual chorus of "chochas," and we kept on walking like we heard nothing.

"What have you heard? I asked.

"Some pillow talk," said Marsha.

"What are you talking about?" I asked

"I was sleeping in the cabin the other day when I overheard Drew talking to Sabra. At least, I pretended to be asleep. I heard him tell Sabra that Rita and her boyfriend were history."

I stopped Marsha in the middle of the path to look her in the eyes.

I said, "There are so many questions I have for you right now, none of which I want to ask in the staff dining room."

"You want to ask them now?"

"We can't be within earshot of anyone when I ask you those questions. This is very delicate, Marsha. And what kind of an idiot is Drew to discuss anything having to do with Rita with Sabra? He's a security guard, for Christ's sake. He ought to know better."

"You would think so," Marsha agreed. "But, you know, Sabra didn't know Rita."

"What's that got to do with anything? You never met Rita either. If Drew knows anything about this case, he shouldn't be discussing it with any of us. It only puts us at more risk. I don't want any involvement in this. I just want to get through Labor Day weekend and get my ass back to school in one piece. Were Susie and Mary-Ann in the cabin when Drew was blabbing about Rita and Rocco?"

"No, it was just me."

"Did you say anything to Susie and Mary-Ann?"

"No," said Marsha. "Stop yelling."

"I'm whispering," I hissed.

"It sounds like you're yelling."

I calmed myself down, and Marsha and I resumed our walk down the path. I maneuvered her under a large maple tree, and said, "Tell me exactly what you heard."

"I told you already. Drew said that Rita and Rocco were history. I had just woken up, and those were the first words I heard."

"What was Sabra's reaction?"

"If she said anything, I didn't hear it. I was still buried under my blanket, with the pillow halfway over my head."

"Do you think that she and Drew are involved in this somehow?"

"Could be," said Marsha. "Oh my God, are we sleeping next to murderers?"

"Have any bodies turned up?" I asked.

"Not yet, but what does 'history' mean?" said Marsha, her eyes wide.

"It sounds to me like they're gone, but not necessarily dead," I said. "Let's not jump the gun."

"You have a way with words, you know that?" said Marsha.

"Anyway," I said, "until we hear something conclusive, I'm going to just mind my own business. Has anything happened on Clarice's case? Do you think that the two cases are related somehow?"

"Well," said Marsha, "I *do* know that heroin is somehow related to Rita's case. But Clarice's? No way, unless Denny was fooling around with drugs."

I looked at her, and said, "Some middle-aged golfer in pink pants involved with heroin? I seriously doubt it. I think that poor Clarice was a victim of circumstance. She picked a jerk for a boyfriend, and he'll go down for assault and probably lose his family. But drugs, no. The other part, about her being tossed into the woods and robbed, that's another story. What do we actually know about Drew and Sabra?"

"I don't know anything about Drew, except he's cute and carries a gun in his pants," Marsha chuckled. "Sabra came in right after Rita left, like me, but she pretty much keeps to herself and her gang of boyfriends. She doesn't mind putting out for petty cash, that's for sure."

Not wanting to be too late for breakfast, I propelled Marsha toward the staff dining room and continued our chat.

75

"So, Sabra would do anything for money, right?" I said.

"It certainly seems that way," said Marsha.

"And Susie and Mary-Ann are completely clueless?" I asked.

"Well, they certainly would be more concerned about Clarice than they would be about Rita," said Marsha. "Nobody really knew Rita. Did you?"

"No," I said, "I really didn't. But I was a little intrigued by her. I mean, the whole Rocco and wig thing. Looked like a set-up, you know? Like she never really belonged. And the business about our tips disappearing? That seemed like a smokescreen to me, especially after Rita disappeared. I'm thinking that someone else was grabbing our tips, while Rita was going for a much bigger score. But there's got to be a much larger story behind it, don't you think?"

"I think we should have a conversation with Susie and Mary-Ann and get their opinions," said Marsha as we entered the staff dining room.

"Are you going to report what you heard Drew tell Sabra?" I asked.

"I really should," said Marsha. "But I'm scared, you know. I open my mouth, and the next thing you know, *I'm* history."

"I'll protect you," I said, smiling. "Or, Mark will. I'm going to have him sleep over a lot more."

We sat down at our table, and Marsha asked, "Speaking of Mark, what's going on with him?"

"He wants me to marry him and have his babies," I said.

"That bastard!" Marsha joked. "Are you interested?"

"Not really," I said. "Does that make me a bad person? I mean, I love Mark, but I have work to do before I settle down and think about the whole family thing. I'm not sure I even want that."

"You'd better use birth control," said Marsha. "You know Mark. He's a stud."

"Don't I know it," I said.

Just then, Leo lumbered over to our table, order pad in hand.

He fixed his gaze on me, and said, "Welcome back, Mrs. Rockefeller. What would you like to drink?"

"I'll have the sauerkraut juice, Leo," I said.

76

"We are all out of sauerkraut juice, Mrs. Rockefeller. I'll bring you orange juice, and some nice eggs with onions, and a toasted bialy.

"That'll be perfect, Leo. Just perfect."

# CHAPTER 24

Rita put her kimono back on and paced the floor of the hotel. She put her hand in her pocket to make sure the pink envelope was still there.

"What kind of extra job do you want me to do?" she asked Rocco, who had gotten out of bed, wrapped a towel around his waist, and sat on the easy chair by the window. "I'm already in too deep as it is. The trafficking job you had me do was Mob-related. You think I don't know that?"

"Keep your voice down," Rocco said.

Rita lowered her voice to a whisper, and hissed, "I'm not an idiot. My ex is a Mobster. I'm sure you know that. He was pissed off that I took some of his money before I left him. Well, he owed me. I did everything for him, but when I found out he was connected, I wanted out."

Rocco knew that more was coming. He waited for Rita to finish.

"He wanted me to have his children, but I wasn't interested. I just wanted to get as far away from him as possible. He thought I owed him something. Fine. I became his drug mule for a couple of weeks, but now I'm done. I've paid my debt."

Rocco got up from his chair and walked over to her. Rita's eyes grew wide, even though his walk was slow and nonthreatening. When he was directly in front of her, he reached out and took her in his arms. She stiffened, but then relaxed into his embrace.

"Rita," he said, "listen to me. Marty's a small fish. We did this job for him."

"What do you mean, 'we'?" said Rita, looking up into his eyes.

"I got you that job at Hoffman's to take care of Marty. Yes, I know your ex. He was planning to bump you off."

Rita gasped and pushed away from him. He pulled her back and continued talking.

"I also have a debt," he said, "to a much bigger fish."

"Oh, no," said Rita. "So, you want to use me to repay it?"

"One more job, baby, and I'm going straight. Honest. Then we can both get out of here and start a new life elsewhere, away from the hoods."

Rita looked up at Rocco, tearfully.

"What about my nephew?"

"Not to sound cold, but your nephew is your cousin's responsibility. We'll give him a nice chunk of change, and he can arrange for his son's care. You can't make a whole life out of living in your cousin's garage and nursing his sick kid between jobs. You're young yet, but not that young if you want to have your own family."

Rita moved away from Rocco and sat on the edge of the bed, considering her options.

"How much are you into them for?"

"Not much," said Rocco. "One more job should more than do it. One nice score, and we're done."

"And if we get caught?" Rita asked.

"Then, we're *really* done," Rocco smiled. "But you know how to do this, baby. You're a real pro. And I mean that in the best possible way."

He pulled Rita up and kissed her on the forehead.

"You're a sweet-talker," Rita said. "Tell me. What exactly do you do when you're not trafficking drugs for the Mob? What kind of a life are we going to have after this?"

Rocco cradled her face in his hands, and said, "I'm a CPA. Whaddya think I am? I'm a professional gambler, all right? That's how I make my money. I play poker. And sometimes I play the horses. I had a losing streak and got a little behind with the loan sharks."

"So, what are you going to do when we end up in – where, Wisconsin?"

"I'll be a farmer," he said with a grin. "Dontcha worry about me. I always land on my feet. I have connections."

"Yeah, Rita interjected, "with a bunch of thugs."

"Listen," Rocco said, "I'll paint houses if I have to. I'll sell cars. I have skills."

"You're not married or anything, are you?" asked Rita.

"Hell, no, baby, of course I'm not. I love you, you know that? I mean, we haven't been together very long, but I really love you. You're tough. And you're beautiful. And you come through for people."

Rita wondered if he was being sincere or if he was merely trying to save his own life. She ran her hands through his exquisite silver hair, and said, "You're bad for me, Rocco, just like every other man I've been with in my life. I'm thinking this won't go well. But I'd be lying if I said I didn't care for you. I'd like to believe we can both have a decent life. I can't say I've ever had a decent life, except for the time I've spent with my cousin and his family. They're good people. I don't want to ever hurt them. But you're right, I can't make that my whole life. "

Rocco kissed Rita firmly on the lips, and said, "Once this is over, I won't let you down, baby. We've both had shady pasts, I know that. But that don't mean we can't have a decent future together. And, if you do this last job for me, we'll both be debt-free, and we can find that new life together. I don't care if it's in Canada."

Rita allowed Rocco to back her up to the bed. He lied down on top of her, and said, "Do this for me, and you'll never have to worry about being alone and broke again. I'll be there for you, like you've been there for me."

As Rita sank beneath Rocco's weight, she tried to envision a life with this man. They were both in their mid-thirties, young enough to have a good, full life together. But she had made bad choices in the past, and she wondered how two petty criminals could start a good life on the spoils of a drug deal.

She also wondered if it was time to reach for the golden ring. Maybe her luck was on the verge of changing for the better.

When their love was spent, Rita got up to use the bathroom. After she locked the door behind her, her hand went to the pink envelope. There was nothing written on the outside, and she carefully tore it open. Her fingers trembled as she removed the note. The words inside were straightforward, but inexplicable.

"I owe you," it said.

There was no signature.

# CHAPTER 25

On the night I returned to work, Ariti took me by the arm and asked if he could see me in his office for a few minutes. How could I refuse?

We both sat down, and he asked, "How are you, Amy? Is everything all right with you? I hope that your personal matter was resolved in the best possible way."

"Thank you, Mr. Ariti. It's so nice of you to ask."

I hoped he wasn't going to ask what the matter was. I didn't relish telling him that I had had a pregnancy scare. Plus, Mark didn't need to further his reputation as the Johnny Wadd of the Catskills. He was still my boyfriend, after all.

Ariti looked at me expectantly, so I made up a little story.

"My grandmother wasn't feeling well, so Mark kindly drove me into the city to visit her for a couple days."

I would have to tell Mark, so he could corroborate my fib, if asked.

"Very nice," said Ariti, nodding. "I hope she's feeling better now."

"I think seeing me did her a world of good," I said. "And it was nice for her to meet Mark. Plus, while we were down there, I got to meet his parents."

At least that part was true. Ariti seemed satisfied.

"The summer's almost over," he said. "Do you think you'll come back next summer and maybe over the winter holidays?"

"Sure," I said, happy to get an invitation. "I would be very happy to come back to work here."

"You're an excellent waitress, Amy," Ariti continued. "The customers like you. And I like you. You're smart, you're honest, and you're very good at what you do."

I was enjoying the flattery, but I didn't know where it was going.

"Why, thank you very much, Mr. Ariti. I enjoy the work, and I've met a lot of good people here."

"I'm glad you're happy, Amy. There's another reason I asked to speak to you privately."

Oh, no, I thought. Here it comes.

"Can I speak to you in confidence, Amy? Can I trust you?"

"I certainly hope so, Mr. Ariti."

"You and I both know there's some kind of monkey business going on around here, and it seems to be going on around your cabin."

"I can't argue with that."

"The security guards can only do so much," he said. "I know that one of them, Drew, is involved with the redhead. What's her name?"

"Sabra," I said.

"Sabra," he repeated. "I can assure you she won't be getting an invitation to return next year, or any other time. I hire school girls, not whores, you should pardon the expression."

He looked at me apologetically.

"Not a problem, Mr. Ariti."

"Drew and Sabra," he went on, "they should both be fired, but we're close to the end of the season, and I don't want to be shorthanded on Labor Day weekend."

"I understand," I said.

I wondered if I should mention what Marsha told me she overhead Drew telling Sabra about Rita and Rocco being history, but I wanted to hear what Ariti wanted from me first. He clearly wanted something. I didn't want to implicate Marsha in anything without consulting her. Maybe she'd just imagined what she'd heard. She was half asleep and buried in linens, after all. I didn't want to put her at risk.

I said, "Is there anything I can do for you, Mr. Ariti?"

"Yes," he said. "I want you to keep your eyes and ears open in the cabin. Pay particular attention to Sabra and Drew's comings and goings. I know you all work crazy hours, but you are in the best position to observe your roommates' behaviors. I want this to be between you and me. Don't tell the other girls we had this chat. Are you in?"

"Can you tell me what you suspect Sabra and Drew of?" I asked, before accepting his request.

"I would rather not say, right now," he replied. "But I will tell you that we've had a big drug problem here of late and an uptick in petty thefts. You already know that Rita hasn't turned up anywhere yet, and we don't know who attacked Clarice."

"Haven't these cases been turned over to the police?" I asked.

"They have, but you're an insider, Amy. I'm not asking you to spy on all your friends over there. Just observe Sabra and Drew and let me know if you see or hear anything amiss. I don't want the hotel involved in a big scandal, if I can help it. Please help me out here. I will make it worth your while."

"To be honest, Mr. Ariti, I'm not comfortable snooping on people, but, if something seems out of line or threatening, I will definitely let you know. "

"That's all I ask," he said, smiling.

Little did Ariti know how deeply interested I was in the whole sordid affair and how much reconnoitering I was willing to do, on the sly. I just didn't want to get killed in the process. And how much did I actually know about Ariti? But I promised that I wouldn't tell the other waitresses about our talk, and I would keep that promise.

# CHAPTER 26

The next morning, after work, Marsha and I corralled Susie and Mary-Ann at the Mountaintop and asked them if they'd heard anything about Rita and Rocco. The two looked at each other and shook their heads.

"No, we haven't," said Mary-Ann. "Why? Have you heard anything? Has someone found Rita?"

"No, and no," I said.

"Why are you asking?" said Susie.

"Marsha overheard Sabra and Drew talking one afternoon in the cabin, when they thought she was asleep," I said.

"Yeah," Marsha said. "Drew was saying that Rita and Rocco were history. His words, not mine."

"Hmmf," said Mary-Ann. "How would he know?"

"That's the question," I said.

Marsha and I looked across the table at our roommates, and they truly seemed clueless.

"You do know about the heroin in Rita's bag, right?" said Marsha.

"Oh, yeah," said Mary-Ann. "I just figured that Rita came here to sell drugs, make a little money, take a little money, and disappear before anyone was any the wiser." She looked at Susie, and asked, "What did *you* think?"

Susie said, "I didn't give it that much thought at all. She just seemed like an oddball to me. I was glad when she left. I figured good riddance."

We clammed up while the waitress put our roast pork sandwiches and drinks in front of us. She put a jar of spicy mustard on the table and asked if we needed anything else. We told her we were good for now, and she hustled off to the next table. When she was out of earshot, I asked, "Would it interest you to know that we think that Drew and maybe even Sabra are involved?"

I looked at Marsha, and got a confirming nod that we agreed on that point.

Susie said, "Involved how?"

Marsha swallowed a bit of sandwich, and said, "We think they're all in cahoots. "

Susie said, "You mean Rita and Rocco and Sabra and Drew?"

I laughed a little, thinking of the movie *Bob & Carol & Ted & Alice*, but I didn't say anything.

"What's so funny?" asked Mary-Ann.

"Nothing, forget it," I said, taking a swig of ginger ale.

Susie said, "I have to admit, my skin crawls around them. They just seem kind of sleazy; made for each other, you know? But do you think they're dealing drugs with Rita and Rocco?"

"I think they might be distributing drugs that Rita delivers to them. I think that Rocco gets the heroin and passes it along to Rita, who gives it to Drew, who passes it along to Sabra. I wouldn't put it past Sabra to prostitute herself for a few extra bucks while she's delivering the heroin and picking up cash from – who? Employees? Guests? There are several thousand people at this resort. Somehow, Sabra receives payment for the drugs, probably takes a cut for herself and Drew, and gives the rest to Rita, who brings it back to Rocco. Who is the final recipient? I'm guessing someone pretty high up in the Mob."

Susie nearly choked on her Dr. Pepper. She sputtered, "Wow! You've got this whole thing figured out! But how can you prove any of it?"

Mary-Ann just stared at me in disbelief, and asked, "You're planning on getting involved with the Mob?"

"Hell, no," I said. "I definitely do not want to get myself whacked before starting my sophomore year of college. That would be foolish."

We all agreed on that and took another bite.

"But wouldn't it be interesting to get to the bottom of this?" I said. "I mean, it sounds like Rita and Rocco may have already gotten whacked, which means that Drew and Sabra might be out of a job. I'll be interested to see how long they stick around."

"Maybe Rita and Rocco are peddling their fish elsewhere," said Marsha.

"Rita could turn up at another hotel, sure," I said. "Different wig, maybe."

We all chewed on that for a few moments.

Finally, Mary-Ann asked, "Do you think this has anything to do with what happened to Clarice?"

"I haven't gotten that far yet," I said. "Does anyone have any thoughts on that matter?"

"I don't know," said Susie. "Sabra was with us right here when Clarice got attacked on the way back to the cabin. She didn't want to go with us when we reported Clarice missing, though. She just went to sleep, remember? And, when we got back, Marsha's tips were missing. Drew didn't show up until after all that. Right? How long has he actually been working here?"

"I think he's kind of a newcomer," I said.

The waitress asked if we were ready for the check. It was time to pay up and go home. We took care of the bill and headed back up the hill. It was about 5 a.m., and we were all exhausted. Our shoes dangled from all of our hands as we walked in the grass beside the path that led to the cabin. Nobody hissed obscenities at us from the shadows, for a change. Maybe Gordie had told the horny dishwashers to shut the hell up.

Charlie was sitting on the porch, as usual. We were too tired to babble, so we said our goodnights. But Charlie stopped us before we entered the cabin.

"I'm only counting four of you girls," he said. "Where's the redhead?"

"She told us she was going to sleep right after work," Marsha said.

"I've been sitting here all night," said Charlie. "Nobody went in there. I figured you were all together. You always head down to that café."

"Damnit," I said, turning the knob.

We all went in, and, sure enough, Sabra wasn't there.

"Maybe she's with Drew," said Charlie.

"Maybe call him on your walkie-talkie and find out," I said.

# CHAPTER 27

Drew picked up, and said, "Drew here."

Charlie opened with, "Is Sabra with you?"

"Yeah, she's right here. What's the matter?"

"She told the other girls she was going to go to sleep after work. That's why she passed on the Mountaintop."

"She did go to sleep," said Drew. "With me. You have a problem with that?"

"Maybe you haven't noticed, but girls have been disappearing around here lately. Sabra tells the others she's going to sleep, they expect to see her in her own bed, as usual. Since when is she going to your place?"

"What business is that of yours?"

"It's my business to keep an eye on these girls until my shift ends at 7 a.m. That's when your ass is supposed to be here, watching these girls; not screwing off with one of them."

Drew said, "Unless my watch is wrong, it's only a few minutes after 5 a.m. That gives me a couple of hours to do whatever the hell I want, with whoever I want."

"All right, all right, calm down," said Charlie. "We were all worried, that's all. Can I talk to Sabra for a minute?"

"She's sleeping, man."

"How about waking her up?"

"Not doing it. How about I just bring her back to the cabin with me when I sign in for my shift."

"I'll be waiting for you," said Charlie.

"You do that," said Drew. "10-4."

"10-4," said Charlie.

—

We all washed up and got into our beds. We were really too exhausted to discuss the matter intelligently, but were too wired to sleep. I could hear everyone tossing and turning.

"Is anyone awake?" whispered Marsha.

"We all said, "Yes.""

"What do you think?" said Marsha. "Do you think Sabra and Drew are going to show up at 7, or do you think they're crossing state lines right now?"

"I hope to be sleeping at 7," said Susie, yawning.

"Let's all try to get some sleep," I said. "I have a feeling that today is going to be a busy day."

"What if they don't show up?" asked Mary-Ann.

"Well, then we'll know that something is rotten in Denmark," I said.

If they didn't show up, then I personally wouldn't have anything to report to Ariti. Charlie would tell Mike, and Mike would tell Ariti. Then the police would be all over the place again. It would be Marsha's prerogative to tell them what she overheard Drew telling Sabra about Rita and Rocco. I had watched enough court TV to know that repeating something that someone else says is hearsay. I could only speak from my own experience. I had a half a mind to wrap things up before Labor Day and head home early, but I wondered if that would cast suspicion on me.

"Sleep tight," I said, putting an arm over my eyes.

But I lay there awake, with thoughts going in circles in my head. I start to lay out a roadmap. First, Rita shows up, and our tips start disappearing. Then, Rita disappears, possibly with her boyfriend, Rocco. Then, her cousin shows up, and he seems clueless about Rita's life outside of his own home. Then, Marsha and Sabra show up. Sabra is sleeping with everyone until she takes up with Drew the security guard. But Drew isn't brought in until after Clarice gets assaulted by her boyfriend, Denny, and then attacked and robbed outside of the cabin. Clarice doesn't see who attacked her, but says the assailant may have smelled like perfume. Hmmm. Maybe a woman? Or maybe a man who had been with a woman?

All of a sudden, we have two security guards watching us: Charlie all night and Drew all day, when he isn't screwing Sabra. Marsha discovers that her tip money has disappeared from the bureau after Rita had left the scene. We could have suspected Sabra, who was in the cabin when we weren't, but she knew where the rest of us were hiding our own money in the closet, and that was untouched. So, that's a dead end. Maybe.

Then, I go away with Mark for a few days, and Marsha tells me she'd overheard Drew telling Sabra that Rita and Rocco are history. Did she dream that up? If not, how does Drew know?

Ariti asks me to spy on Drew and Sabra, acknowledging there are drug, theft, and assault problems at the resort, and that the cocktail waitresses seem to be in the thick of it: victims, and maybe perpetrators. Ariti dangles another summer's work in front of me like a carrot, along with other implied financial benefits if I report to him all activity having to do with Sabra and Drew. I pretty much tell him I don't want to be a rat, but agreed to be observant.

Susie and Mary-Ann are clueless. They're finishing out their summer at Hoffman's with their middle-aged boyfriends, afternoons at the lake, and hustling for tips all night. That's what Ariti always says to us at the beginning of our shifts: "Hustle." And we do.

And then, Sabra goes missing with Drew, who is due back at the cabin at 7 a.m.

I reach into my end table and feel for the napkin I have Lovato's number written on. It's still there, and I think about going to the phone booth in the main lobby and calling him in the morning. Maybe Rita's been in touch with him. Maybe he knows something he isn't telling anybody. I wonder who's taking care of his kid, and who's minding the store.

And then, I fall into a dead sleep.

I awaken to a beehive of activity a few hours later.

Rita and Rocco aren't necessarily dead. But Sabra and Drew are.

# CHAPTER 28

W ake up," said Marsha, shaking me gently.
"What's happening?" I asked, groggily, still embroiled in a dream.

I opened my eyes and saw all of my roommates looking down on me. They all had very somber looks on their faces. I pushed myself up with my elbows behind me and looked from one to the other.

"What's going on, and what time is it?" I asked, squinting at the radio alarm clock on the end table. It was a few minutes after 10 a.m.

"I didn't want to wake you," said Marsha. "You were so sound asleep, but they're throwing us out of the cabin again."

"Who's throwing us out?" I asked, looking around.

"Ariti is sending us back to the hotel," said Marsha.

"Does this have something to do with Rita and Rocco being history?" I asked.

"No, it has something to do with Sabra and Drew being history," said Mary-Ann.

"What does that mean?" I said, throwing my feet onto the floor. "What the hell happened? Did they not make it back here at 7 a.m.?"

"They didn't make it back here at all," said Susie. "They were found dead in Drew's car between here and Monticello."

"Was there an accident?" I asked.

"Well, if they accidentally got shot between the eyes, then, yes, it was an accident," said Marsha, wryly.

"Jesus," I said. "That has 'Mob hit' written all over it. Get me the hell outta here!"

"We're all getting the hell outta here," said Mary-Ann. "We're going back to the suite with the big bathtub. It got freed up, and we'll be in it for the rest of the summer – or until we get bumped off."

"Not funny," I said.

"Mike came to the door earlier with our marching orders," said Susie. "We're supposed to clear all of our own stuff out, but not touch the

90

drawer where we used to keep our tips, and not go near Sabra's bed or personal belongings. They're giving us until noon to get our stuff together before they descend upon the place with the police. Say good-bye to your window, Amy."

"The suite has all the windows I need," I said.

"What a summer," sighed Mary-Ann.

"It's more than I bargained for, that's for sure," I said.

I pulled my suitcase out of the closet and put it on my bed, just to get myself started.

"I'm going to take a shower to wake myself up a little more," I announced.

The others had already gotten dressed and were busily packing their meager possessions. I don't know how I slept through who-knows-what-kind of commotion. Maybe I was just dragging from the whole week, and, once I got into the bathroom, I noticed that my late period had finally arrived. Great.

We were all ready to move by the time noon rolled around. We didn't need to trudge to the main house carrying our bags like refugees. Mike put our bags into his station wagon and told us he would deliver them to our room.

"We'll just about have time to get things organized before we have to report to work tonight," said Marsha as we strolled toward our new digs. "Do you think that reporters will be swarming around the hotel, or just the cops?"

"I'm pretty sure that the hotel is doing whatever it can to keep from becoming front-page news," I said.

"Yeah, but they're not going to have any choice," said Marsha. "News just came out about a hitman going away for life for a shooting on 17 a year ago. The press is going to have a field day with another apparent Mob hit on the same road. The hotel is not going to be able to hide the fact that the two latest victims worked here and that they were probably involved in a drug trafficking ring."

"You're right," I said. "When we're questioned, will you tell the police about what you overheard Drew telling Sabra about Rita and Rocco?"

91

"I'll tell them as long as long as they don't identify me as a source in the newspapers," said Marsha. "I don't want to get involved in this mess. I'll tell you one thing, though. If my father hears about this, he'll be up here in a red-hot minute to take me home."

"Probably not just yours," I said.

"It *has* been a pretty exciting summer," said Susie. "I wish I could tell you we didn't have Mob activity in sleepy Binghamton, but I'd be lying."

"I live on Long Island, the capitol of wise guys!" I said.

We all chuckled a little, except for Mary-Ann who was fretting over whether her boyfriend was connected or not.

"Fuhgeddaboudit," said Susie, using one of Mary-Ann's favorite expressions. "You'll be heading back to the Cape soon. You will leave your guy behind, just as I will leave mine behind. This is the capitol of the summer fling."

We all nodded in agreement. Susie was a woman of the world now, not the innocent waif she was at the beginning of the summer.

"I wonder if this is going to cut down on the crowds expected for Labor Day weekend," I ruminated.

Marsha said, "I doubt it. The Mafia is all over the place, these days. Some schnook from Queens in a Jeep Wagoneer with a wife and a passel of kids isn't going to be the target of some goombah looking to settle a score in Ferndale."

"You sound very tough for a Jewish girl from Richmond, you know that?" I said. "What do *you* know about goombahs?"

"I saw *The Godfather* last year," she said. "I know things. And Richmond isn't crime-free. We're not all just a bunch of simpletons with magnolias in our hair."

She gave me a hurt, but somehow superior, look.

I rolled my eyes, and said, "I never said you were. And, since you know things, doesn't the FBI get involved when there's Mob-related activity?"

"I'm pretty sure they do," said Marsha. "Maybe they'll send J. Edgar Hoover."

"Wow, you *do* know stuff," I said. "But, nope. I think he retired recently. Too bad."

"At the very least, we may get some answers before the summer season closes in a couple of weeks," Marsha said.

"Sophomore year is going to seem very tame after this," I said.

# CHAPTER 29

I ferreted out some change and called Lovato on the pay phone in the lobby. A woman answered. I assumed it was Lovato's wife.

"Hello," I said. "Is this the Lovato residence?"

"Yes, it is," said the voice.

"Is this Mrs. Lovato?"

"No. Mr. and Mrs. Lovato are at work. May I ask who's calling?"

"This is Amy from Hoffman's Resort. I used to work with Mr. Lovato's cousin, Rita."

The phone went silent for a moment, and I thought maybe the person at the other end had hung up. Then, she spoke again.

"I'm just a caretaker here," she said. "You may want to call back this evening. Or, if this is urgent, you may try them at the store. I have a number for them."

I asked her to hold on for a moment while I bolted over to the front desk to get a pad and pen. I practically dove back into the phone booth and closed the glass door.

I said, "I am ready for the number," and she gave it to me.

"May I have your name, please?" I asked. "I want to be able to tell Mr. Lovato how I got his work number."

"It's Doris," came the reply.

I said, "Doris, can you please tell me if Mr. Lovato's cousin, Rita, has been at the house in the past few days?"

"I couldn't say," said Doris. "I come at 8 a.m. and leave at 5 p.m. I haven't seen anyone come or go since I've started working here. If someone comes at night, I wouldn't know about it. I'm just here to take care of the boy during the day."

"Thank you, Doris. You've been a great help. I'll call Mr. Lovato at the store now."

"You're welcome, Amy. Is that what you said your name is?"

"Yes, I'm Amy. Thanks, again."

94

I disconnected and blew out some air. I didn't want to alarm Lovato. I just wanted to find out if he'd heard from Rita. It seemed an innocent enough question coming from a concerned former coworker. He had given me his home phone number, after all. I collected myself and placed the call.

A man answered, "Ellenville Market."

"Is Richard Lovato available?" I asked.

"Yeah, that's me."

"Hello, Mr. Lovato. This is Amy from Hoffman's. We met not long ago. I used to work with Rita."

"Yeah, I remember you. How ya doin'?"

"I'm fine, Mr. Lovato. I told you I might call, and here I am. I was wondering if you ever heard from Rita?"

He didn't even ask me where I got his work number. He didn't act suspicious about why I was calling him. We were just having a normal conversation. I began to relax.

"Yeah, I heard from her a few days ago. She said she and her boyfriend were taking a trip."

"Is she okay?" I asked.

"Yeah," he said. "But I think she's in trouble. The police came by to give me the third degree about her," he said. "I have nothing to hide. I'm an honest businessman with a wife and kid. I told them she was staying with me and my family and working at Hoffman's for a coupla weeks. Then, all of a sudden, she goes missing, and after a few days, I start to look around. That's when I met you and your boss. What's his name? Ariti?"

"That is correct," I said.

"Yeah, so he gives me a bag of Rita's stuff, and I don't think nothing about it until the police take it and find drugs. Some kind of residue. I never woulda noticed. Anyway, I give it to them. No fight from me. I don't know what she's up to, and I don't wanna know. She doesn't have the best past, if you catch my drift. I thought she was all straightened out. And she was good with my kid. So, who doesn't deserve a second chance, right? But now, I don't know what's what."

"Did you tell Rita about your visit from the police?" I asked.

"Yeah, I mentioned the cops and what they found in her bag. She told me she didn't know what I was talking about; that she was clean.

What do I know? But the cops told me to let them know if I hear from her, so I let them know. I just couldn't tell them where she was calling from. She told me to find someone else to watch Tommy for a coupla weeks, and then she'd be back, same as before. She just needed a little time with her guy, you know?"

"Rocco?"

"Yeah, who else? I still never met the guy but, if she likes him, what can I say?"

I was a little concerned about staying on the phone too long because who knew if the phone was bugged. But, all of a sudden, Lovato came out with, "What kind of a racket is going on at that hotel?"

"What do you mean, Mr. Lovato?"

"I mean, I get the papers. I saw that a coupla Hoffman's employees, including another one of you cocktail waitresses, got killed a few days ago, not far from the hotel. For a minute, I thought it was Rita that got killed, but then I got the call from her, and I knew she was at least alive. The names of the deceased weren't released in the article. But maybe you know who they are."

"I do," I said, "but I'm not at liberty to talk about it."

I was probably at liberty to talk about whatever I wanted to, but I wasn't going to do it over the phone. I apologized to Lovato for not being forthcoming.

"Did Rita say where she and Rocco were going?" I asked.

"Nah. And I didn't ask. She gotta know that the police are interested. Maybe the FBI, if drugs are involved. I don't need any of this."

"I'm sorry about all of it, Mr. Lovato."

"What do *you* have to be sorry about? You didn't do nothing. You're a good kid. Let me give you a piece of advice."

"Okay," I said.

"Go home," he said. "Go to school. Go where it's safe. And don't look back."

# CHAPTER 30

Returning to my, thankfully, empty room, I changed into a bikini and flip flops. I grabbed a towel and suntan lotion and plopped them into a beach bag. I put on a wide-brimmed hat, sunglasses, and a coverup before leaving the hotel because I wanted to be incognito. I had some thinking to do.

One of Mark's buddies spotted me as soon as I showed up. I made idle chitchat with him for a few minutes, but then sent him off and ducked behind a vacant cabana. I told him I wanted to be alone, like Greta Garbo. I let my mind go wild while I baked in the sun with the hat over my face. If someone else recognized me, maybe they would think I was asleep and leave me in peace.

So, it sounded like Rita and Rocco were on the run. I didn't buy that crap about Rita returning to Lovato's house in Ellenville in a couple of weeks for a minute. She and Rocco were definitely on the lam, and maybe for lots of different reasons.

Did I believe they were involved with drug trafficking at Hoffman's? Yes. Did I believe they were teaming up with Sabra and Drew? Very likely. Did I think they were all connected to the Mob? Probably. Did Rita know what she was getting into from the start? Maybe so, maybe not.

And, while I was busy cogitating away, I wondered if Clarice's assault and robbery were in any way related to this devious group. Could they have been connected to someone else who was setting the stage for what was to come? Julius? Ariti? The bimmies? Did someone have an axe to grind with the hotel?

I told myself to get back to grim reality. On the other hand, there was no harm in fantasizing freely. Somehow, I had to get this to all add up.

All of a sudden, I got whacked in the face with a beachball. Good thing my face was covered with a hat, but it soon fell off as I jumped up in surprise.

A little blonde boy in a powder blue swim suit was standing there giggling at me. I could see that his fair skin was turning pink from the sun. I tossed the ball over to him, just as his mother arrived with another, older, child in tow; a girl. The mother was an attractive brunette, maybe in her early thirties, in a gold one-piece.

"Apologize to the lady, Timmy," she said to the kid holding the beachball like a beer belly."

"I'm sorry," he lisped, but he still looked like he was on the verge of laughing.

"That's okay," I said, smiling. "No harm done."

"Sometimes, these children just get away from me," said the mother.

"I can only imagine," I said.

"Are you a guest here?" she asked.

"No," I said. "I work here. I have the afternoon off."

Something told me to not reveal too much about my summer occupation. After my few minutes of deep thinking, I was in a state of mild paranoia.

"That's nice," she said. "My husband used to work here."

"Oh? What did he do?"

"He was one of the golf pros."

I nearly choked, but managed to keep my face placid.

I said, "I don't get to use many of the amenities here, including the golf course. I mainly spend time at the lake, when I'm not working in the dining room. It's so busy this summer."

It wasn't exactly a lie.

"Are you and your husband and kids staying here as guests now?" I asked.

"No husband; just me and the kids," she said. "To tell you the truth, my husband and I are splitting up. He was sinking his balls into too many holes, if you know what I mean," she said, with a sneer.

What else could she mean? From the venom in her tone, I could tell that Denny had a long history of putting his putter where it didn't belong. Poor naïve Clarice.

"Oh, that doesn't sound very nice," I agreed.

I was uncomfortable with her talking like that in front of her children. The little boy was oblivious, but the girl seemed to be getting the gist of what her mother was saying.

"Yeah," she continued, "my husband and I met here at a singles weekend around twelve years ago. I was in my senior year of college and getting ready for law school. Denny was a sexy older man. I fell for him."

Wow. She actually said his name.

I nodded, and said, "That happens a lot around here."

"Anyway," she said, "I'd better get these kids out of the sun. It was nice chatting with you."

She held out her hand, and said, "My name is Gina."

I took her hand, and said, "I'm Amy."

She had quite a grip. And, when she came close, she smelled strongly of something flowery, like Rive Gauche.

She turned to walk away with steering hands on her children's shoulders, but threw me a, "See you around," over her shoulder.

Not if I see you first, I thought. I didn't know how I was going to prove it, but I had a feeling I had just met Clarice's attacker.

# CHAPTER 31

I did share my theory with the girls as we prepared for work late that afternoon. It sounded feasible to them that Denny's spurned wife would lay in wait for Clarice and confront her somehow. But how would she know that Clarice would be walking back to the cabin alone at 4 a.m.? And why would she take Clarice's jewelry and money? We all knew she was a successful lawyer. Maybe she was attempting to put suspicion on someone else.

"Who would have been in a position to tip her off?" asked Marsha.

"Let's think about it," said Susie. "We know that Denny worked here for a long time and that he met his wife here. Maybe she used to come up and stay with him regularly, before her career kicked into high gear. How many employees did she meet and form relationships with?"

"Well, my boyfriend has been here for years, but I wouldn't want to get him wrapped up in this," said Mary-Ann.

"He's been the maître d in the main dining room for years," I said. "Surely, he's met Denny's wife."

"Yes, but what would motivate him to put Clarice in danger?" asked Mary-Ann. "That doesn't make sense."

"No offense, Mary-Ann, but none of us are in love with your boyfriend. We don't like the way he treats you," I said. "Did Clarice ever say anything nasty to him? Is he a vindictive jerk?"

Mary-Ann didn't come running to her boyfriend's defense, but she didn't buy that he had anything to do with Clarice's attack.

"Come up with another theory," she said.

"I turned to Susie, and said, "How about your guy, Susie?"

Susie said, "My guy works with your guy, and they're both good guys. My boyfriend doesn't have a mean bone in his body. And he wasn't any great fan of Denny's, even if we did double date a couple of times. He knew that Denny was married, for one thing."

"Why didn't he speak up?" I asked.

"He didn't think it was his place. He didn't even say anything to me until Denny got fired."

"Swell," I said.

My sarcasm was lost on Susie. But I really didn't think that Susie's boyfriend was involved in Clarice's downfall.

"Who would know about Clarice's schedule?" Marsha asked.

"Just about anyone who works in the dining room, cocktail lounge, or nightclub," said Mary-Ann. "The bartenders would know. Even Mark's ex would know," she said, looking at me. "Did Clarice work the dining room that night?"

"Let me think," I said. "Clarice was feeling pretty lousy that night. She could barely put one foot in front of the other. We didn't know yet that she had been knocked around by that bastard, Denny. And we certainly didn't know she was on the verge of miscarrying. But she was determined to work, remember? I think we all worked in the dining room until around 9 p.m., then headed to the nightclub. We ended up in the cocktail lounge after the show, right? Did anyone overhear Clarice saying that she wasn't going to join us at the Mountaintop?"

We all ruminated for a moment. Who in the world would have a problem with sweet Clarice, aside from Denny himself? He hadn't gotten fired yet. Had he said something to his wife? Was Ariti somehow involved? Was it possible that someone had mistaken Clarice for me? I was also a slender brunette, though not as thin as Clarice.

Did Mark's ex-girlfriend, Jean, intend to kill me and then stopped when she saw that it was Clarice on the ground and not me? Maybe she left Clarice in the woods, and the bimmies – or someone else – came around afterward and took some money and jewelry, after the fact.

Holy shit! Why was I even thinking of sticking around through Labor Day? This place was a snake pit!

Marsha asked, "Do you think this has anything to do with the drug trafficking ring?"

"Actually," I said, "I do not. I think they're isolated incidents that occurred at about the same time. That doesn't mean that I don't think that Rita or Drew or Sabra had something to do with the disappearance of our tips. It may have been a diversion, unless someone was really desperate for money. If someone was indebted to the Mob, then I think they would try to get money however possible. We all make very good money in tips; truly, thousands of dollars a week. Somebody knew that. And somebody knew where we kept our money. And the money didn't start to disappear until Rita showed up."

"And when the rip-off continued, it could have been Sabra or Drew," said Susie.

"That's right," I said. "As a security guard, Drew even had a key to our cabin. He could have let himself in at any time, and nobody would have questioned it."

"Surely, the cops have picked up some evidence by now," said Marsha. "And if the FBI has been involved, the whole place has been swept."

We all nodded in agreement.

"So, Marsha," I said, "I think you should tell the police that you overheard what Drew said to Sabra about Rita and Rocco. Drew and Sabra are dead, so you don't have to worry about any payback from them."

Marsha agreed, and said, "And I think you should tell the police about the conversation you had with Richard Lovato, about Rita returning after a couple of weeks of running with Rocco."

"I will tell them," I said.

"And I think you should have a conversation with Mark about his ex, who has already demonstrated a jealous rage toward you," said Mary-Ann.

"I don't want to get her involved unless it's absolutely necessary," I said.

"Maybe grab a hold of Denny's wife and have a frank conversation about Denny and his relationship with Clarice," said Susie. "She's already initiated a relationship with you, and she's going to be around with her children for the next couple of weeks. Maybe she'll come clean with you."

"Or maybe she'll try to strangle me," I said.

We were ready to discuss things further when a knock came at the door. We gasped, but at least we were dressed.

"Who is it?" Mary-Ann called out.

"It's me, Clarice!"

"Clarice!" we yelled, as we all went running for the door in our high heels.

# CHAPTER 32

W e all took turns hugging Clarice, who looked well-rested and less gaunt than the last time we had seen her. We didn't expect her to return to the mountains so soon. In fact, we never expected to see Clarice again. We asked her where she was staying.

"I'm staying right here with my parents until the lawyers are finished with me," said Clarice. "Mr. Ariti talked to hotel bigwigs about comping us a room until this mess is over."

"It's the least they could do," Marsha said. "You got injured in so many different ways here. I hope it doesn't upset you too much to be back."

"Well, I *would* be upset if I had to see the cabin again, or walk down the path to get there," said Clarice. "Plus, I just found out about all the crazy stuff that went on here after I left. What are all y'all still doing here?"

"We're not all here," I said. "Sabra got killed a few days ago, along with her boyfriend. We think it was Mob-related."

Clarice said, "Yes, they told us about that. Terrible."

"Yes, and we're pretty sure that Rita and Rocco are still out there, running from the law," said Marsha. "I think they'd be better off if the cops caught them before the Mob did."

Clarice nodded and was about to say more when I abruptly stopped her.

"Listen, I said, "we're going to be late for work. There's something you need to know before we send you back to your folks."

Clarice looked at me, warily.

"Denny's wife is here with their kids," I said.

Clarice turned pale.

"How do you know that?" she asked.

"I accidentally met her the other day, down at the lake. I don't have the time to go into detail right now, but make sure you're with your parents at all times. And, if I were you, I'd steer clear of the dining room."

104

"They're guests here?"

"Yes, until the end of Labor Day weekend."

"Is Denny back?"

"No, Denny's not here anymore. I think he's being held somewhere. But I don't trust his wife's presence here at this time. I have reason to believe that she's the one who attacked you on the path."

"How the...?" she began.

"Just go back to your parents, and keep a low profile," I said. "Maybe don't even stay here. Come, we're going to walk you back to your room on our way to the lounge. We'll talk more tomorrow. Where did they put you?"

"Right next door to you," said Clarice.

—

"It doesn't make any sense to me that Ariti would put Clarice up at this hotel when he knows that Denny's wife is staying here," said Susie. "He knows what went down between Denny and Clarice. Why would he risk her having an encounter with his wife?"

"Soon-to-be ex-wife," I said.

"Who cares?" Susie exploded. "Hasn't Clarice already been through enough crap with this place? Why put her in harm's way?"

I reeled off a few possibilities in Ariti's defense.

"Number one, Denny is no longer here, so Clarice is under no threat from him. Number two, while I think that Denny's wife might have been Clarice's attacker, I could very well be wrong. I'm a major speculator, but what do I actually know? Nothing! Number three, Clarice is here with her parents. I doubt Gina's going to want to duke it out with Clarice's father. And, number four, they all want to see Denny in Hell."

"Why is Gina here at all?" asked Mary-Ann.

"She told me she was vacationing with her kids," I said. "I doubt she was counting on her philandering husband's unsuspecting mistress being here at the same time, unless Ariti said something to her."

"Why would Ariti do that?" asked Susie. "What could he possibly stand to gain?"

"I don't know," I said. "How well does Ariti know Gina?"

"Oh, please, let's not cast Mr. Ariti in a bad light," said Mary-Ann. "He's never been anything other than kind to us. And what are you thinking? You think he's having an affair with Gina? So, what? It doesn't look like he has anything resembling a home life. We don't know a thing about the man, really. He appears to live in the cocktail lounge, when he's not in his office. I've never seen him in anything other than a suit. I don't think I've ever seen the man eat! But I don't doubt that he's human. If Denny has a long history of running around on Gina, maybe she has the occasional fling with Mr. Ariti. Big deal! It still doesn't add up that he would want to put Clarice in harm's way. Clarice was a completely innocent bystander. She thought she had a boyfriend, until she announced she might be pregnant. Then, bam! Reality hit hard. Let's not judge Mr. Ariti too harshly."

"I'm not judging him," I said. "I'm just speculating, as usual. I just don't want to see Clarice hurt again."

We entered the lounge to get our table assignments for the night, and there was Ariti, chatting with Gina at his usual table. The kids weren't there. She was alone with him, in a sapphire cocktail dress, laughing up a storm. And her hand was on his arm, comfortably, like it had been there before.

Ariti spotted us as we stood stalled at the entrance of the lounge. He beckoned us in with a smile.

"Hi, girls," he said. "Say 'hello' to my sister, Gina."

# CHAPTER 33

"Oh," said Gina, reaching out a hand as we approached, "I remember this one. We met at the lake. Amy, right?"

She embraced me, and I smelled her Rive Gauche. It was unmistakable, and she had really laid it on. I patted her on her bare back and tried to hold back a sneeze. I'm allergic to most perfumes, and this one was really making my eyes water.

Ariti stated, "So, you girls already know each other."

"Yes, we recently met," I said. "Where are the kids?" I asked Gina.

"Oh, I found them a sitter," said Gina. "Mommy has to get out on her own now and then, especially now. It *is* singles weekend, and I *am* single."

She smiled, a little bitterly, I thought.

"Not yet," said Ariti.

"Did any of you know my husband, Denny?" she asked.

We all looked down at our shoes. Surely, Gina knew that Clarice was not among us at that moment. But I didn't mention Clarice. I simply said, "We knew of him."

Ariti interrupted the conversation with, "Okay, ladies. It's singles weekend, as my sister just pointed out. This is the time to really hustle. It'll be the last singles weekend before Labor Day. It won't be a family crowd. The singles like to drink. It loosens them up. Makes the conversations less awkward."

We had experienced a couple of other singles weekends that summer, and it was when we made our best money. Ariti gave us our station assignments, and sent us off with another, "Get out there and hustle." I could feel Gina's eyes following us as we ran off to work ourselves into a stupor.

When we were out of earshot, Marsha said, "Maybe we should all be running for our lives."

"Why would you say that?" asked Susie. "Gina has no reason to have it in for any of us."

"Did you see that dress she was wearing?" asked Mary-Ann.

"Who could miss it?" said Marsha. "She was gorgeous in it. She's going to be beating them off with a stick tonight."

"As long as she doesn't go after anyone else with that stick," I said.

"I'm going to be a little late for work," said Susie. "Mary-Ann, can you cover for me for a few minutes? I need to go back upstairs and warn Clarice about Gina."

"Let *me* go," I said to Susie. "I'm covered in Gina's perfume. I want to see if it brings back any memories."

Susie abruptly grabbed a hold of me and squeezed me in her arms.

She backed up, and said, "Do *I* smell like Gina now?"

"Well, yeah," I grimaced. "The whole building is going to end up smelling like Gina."

Susie ran off before I could say another word, and I stood there sneezing uncontrollably. It actually was more appropriate that Susie speak with Clarice. They were very close before Clarice's mishaps and subsequent return to Dallas. But this gave me the brief opportunity to speak with the others before the thirsty throngs showed up.

I started with, "Do you think that Ariti invited his sister and Clarice at the same time intentionally, or do you think it was just a coincidence?"

"How would we know?" asked Mary-Ann. "What would motivate him to do that?"

"I think he's a protective big brother," I said. "I think he wants to have Gina make amends with Clarice before she gets arrested for assault and robbery, and Clarice presses charges. I mean, it was Denny who did the most harm, and he should go away for it. He's the one who put Clarice in the hospital, not Gina. Gina just laid her out in the woods."

"Yeah, but first she gave Clarice the Vulcan nerve pinch," said Marsha. "And then she took her money and jewelry, don't forget. She has a lot of explaining to do, don't you think? Clarice could have been eaten by wild animals or bled out in those woods. Don't give Gina too much of a pass on all this, Amy. Clarice is the injured party here. And maybe Gina should pay for her part of it – that is, if she actually is the one who attacked Clarice on the path."

"You're right," I said. "I don't know why I'm so willing to let Gina off so easily, if she's the perpetrator."

"Let's just see how this all unfolds," said Mary-Ann.

She then pointed to the crowd gathering on the other side of the soon-to-be unlocked glass double doors of the dining room. It was nearly 5 p.m., and it was time for the singles to stampede in. You would think they hadn't eaten in a month.

—

Clarice's father opened the door to Susie, and said, "Yes? Can I help you?"

Susie introduced herself, and Clarice came to the door.

"Let her in, Daddy," she said.

Susie gave Clarice a hug, and Clarice backed up.

"What in the world have you bathed yourself in?" she asked.

"It's perfume. Do you recognize the scent?"

"Yes," said Clarice, fanning her face. "It's Rive Gauche. Everyone's wearing it this year. Lord, that's loud! Why are you wearing so much of it?"

"Do you remember smelling it the night you were attacked?"

Clarice's face fell with the memory. "Yes, that was it," she said.

"This is Denny's wife's perfume I'm wearing," said Susie.

Clarice gave her a perplexed look, and said, "Why?"

"It's a long story, and I don't have but a few minutes. I just wanted to let you know something, really quick. We just found out that Gina is Ariti's sister. I don't know why you and his sister are here at the same time, but I feel like something's on the verge of happening."

Clarice's mother spoke up from a chair by the window.

"What's happening?" she asked. "Is my girl in danger again?"

"No, Mrs. O'Hare," Susie said. "We're all going to keep your girl safe. I just had a juicy bit of gossip for Clarice to chew on. And, speaking of chewing, I'd go somewhere else for dinner tonight. It's singles weekend, and it's going to be a madhouse in the dining room."

Susie whispered to Clarice, "You may want to keep all this under your hat for a little while. We don't want to wrongly accuse anybody. But I think we're on the right track. I've got to run. I'll see you tomorrow. Don't worry about anything."

And she was gone.

But Clarice knew something that Susie didn't know, and not only Susie. Nobody had given her a moment to speak. If they had, she would have told them that Ariti had returned her money and pilfered possessions to her in a paper bag earlier that day.

# CHAPTER 34

Rocco drove the Pinto into a dark cul de sac a couple of blocks away from the Lovato house. It was a steamy night. Rocco parked the car beneath an elm tree drooping with rain. He and Rita sat in silence for a moment. Then, Rocco rolled his window down an inch and asked Rita to do the same. She wordlessly obeyed.

"Damn hot tonight," he said.

Rita sat looking out the windshield, like they were still on the highway. She barely blinked. The shock of what she had witnessed had rendered her mute. Rocco sat with his hands on the wheel, prepared to leave at any moment.

"I'm sorry you had to see that, baby," he said.

Rita continued to stare out the window into the wet leaves of the elm. The wig she was told to wear for the meet felt like an anvil on her head. Sweat poured down her forehead, the salt burning her eyes.

"We were lucky, you know," said Rocco. "If we got to the meet a few minutes earlier, we would've gotten hit, too. This way, we saw what we saw and kept on going. There are rival gangs, you know. It's hard to know who's on who's turf around here, you know? These things happen sometimes."

Rita sat quietly, chewing on her bottom lip, her hands neatly folded in her lap.

"Talk to me," said Rocco.

Rita turned to him, and said, "What's there to talk about? We just saw two people get shot in the head. We're next, right?"

Rocco put one of his hands atop Rita's and kept the other one on the wheel. His eyes darted from his rearview mirror to his sideview mirror and back to Rita. He spoke to her from his heart.

"Listen," he said, "when I first met you and knew you had a past, I figured you were the ideal partner in crime for me."

Rita huffed at the expression.

Rocco continued, "We were both in debt to some very bad guys. We were able to pay yours off with that job at Hoffman's. And we were on our way to getting the last installment, which woulda made it easier for me to pay off mine. But it didn't work out that way, you know?"

Rita nodded, and said, "Yeah, I know. So, now the sharks send a hitman for you?"

"Nah," said Rocco. "Oh, maybe to rough me up a little, but if they kill me, they'll never get their money back, and that's what they really want. It's all business with them, you know? Those guys like me, personally. I get them plenty of business. So, I'll give them what I've got, and I'll get another week or two to come up with the rest. And, you know what, baby? I'll do it."

Rita started to cry, "And what if you don't?"

"You let me worry about that because, as of now, you're out."

Rita looked at Rocco, and said, "What do you mean, I'm out? You don't need me anymore?"

"Oh, I need you, all right, but not to put your life in danger. I've endangered you enough as it is. I may even go to one shark to get enough to pay off the other shark, and that'll buy me more time. Maybe I'll have a winning streak at poker. Who knows? But I'm leaving you here at the curb. You go back to your cousin. It's a short walk."

"I want to stay with you," said Rita.

"We ain't no *Bonnie and Clyde*," joked Rocco. "I told you. I love you. That means I need to protect you. When all this blows over, I'll come for you. We'll both be out of debt, and we'll go to fucking Kansas."

Rita shook her head, like she had her doubts. She looked out the window and considered her options. There was a steady rain now, and she didn't have an umbrella.

"It's almost 11 at night," she said. "What am I supposed to do, just show up at my cousin's door, like a waif? Maybe he won't even let me in. Then, what'll I do? Walk the streets until the Mob picks me off?"

Rocco couldn't help but laugh.

He said, "I'll be lurking in the shadows on the other side of the street. If he doesn't take you in, I'll pick you up and bring you to a motel somewhere. Now, take off that wig and glasses. You look like an old

112

librarian, and I've never been that great of a reader. I want to kiss you goodbye."

Rita's face crumpled. She said, "Don't put it that way."

"I want to kiss you goodnight," he rephrased.

Rita removed the glasses and unclipped the wig from her head. She shook her head to tousle her hair and reached for Rocco. He took her in his arms over the gear shift and kissed her slow and deep.

"Tell me that everything's going to be all right," she whispered.

Rocco spoke to her reassuringly, then said, "Listen, if the cops come looking for you, I want you to sell me out. Tell them I got you into this racket, because it's true. I don't want you to try to save me. I want you to save yourself and protect your family. Promise me."

Rita promised, but didn't mean it.

"What are you going to do with the wig and glasses?" she asked.

"They'll be on the bottom of the Hudson by midnight," he said.

# CHAPTER 35

Rita took one last look at Rocco before she opened the car door and stepped out into the rain. Fortunately, it was a misting rain and not a downpour. If Rocco was behind her, he was moving so slowly she didn't hear him. She walked quickly along the sidewalk, crossing the road to avoid streetlamps. Finally, she walked up the porch steps to get to Lovato's front door. There were two small lamps dimly illuminating the small entry and a trellis on each side with tendrils of vines and roses climbing through them. She rang the doorbell.

A light went on in the foyer. Rita could see Lovato peeking out from behind the living room curtains. He had a surprised look on his face and quickly left the window to open the door. In the few seconds it took for him to do so, Rocco vacated the short block. If Lovato sent her away, Rita hoped that Rocco wasn't far off.

"Where the hell you been?" asked Lovato.

Without giving her a chance to answer, he grabbed Rita by the arm and pulled her into the foyer.

"You're soaking wet, for Christ's sake," he said. "We didn't know if you were dead or alive. You hear about those kids who got killed earlier? We heard about it on the 9 o'clock news. Their names weren't released. We were afraid it was you."

Lovato grabbed Rita to give her a hug and found her shivering.

"Can I tell you all about it in the morning, Richie?" she asked. "It's been a hell of a day. I need to take a hot shower and sleep. Then I'll tell you everything."

"Are you hungry?" Lovato asked. "We have leftover lasagna."

Rita hadn't thought about food and realized that she was starving.

"I'm famished," she said.

"Let me go warm some up for you," said Lovato, leading her into the kitchen by the hand, as if she didn't know where the kitchen was.

Lovato's wife yelled down the staircase, "Is everything all right down there?"

"Yeah, Marie," he yelled back. "Go back to bed. I'll be up soon."

"It's late," she yelled again. "Who is it?"

"Just go back to bed, already," he said. "I'll tell you when I come up."

Rita fell more than sat down on a kitchen chair as Lovato bustled around.

"You don't look so good," he said. "And what happened to all your hair?"

"I cut and colored it," Rita said. "Please, Richie, no questions until tomorrow morning. It's been a terrible day, and I'm dead on my feet. All I want to do is eat a little, take a shower, and sleep. I'll tell you everything in the morning, I promise. And thank you so much for taking me in. I don't know what I'd do without you."

"Are you kidding?" he said. "We've been worried sick about you. You're in trouble with the police, you know that?"

Lovato ran out of the kitchen while the lasagna was heating in the microwave and came back in with a thick towel and a fluffy robe from the laundry room.

"Get out of those wet clothes and dry yourself off before you eat. You'll get sick. You have two minutes before the food is ready. Go."

Rita took the towel and robe and dried off in the laundry room. She threw her wet clothes into the laundry basket on top of the washer before returning to the kitchen. A plate of pasta was already on the table, and Lovato had poured her a glass of Grappa.

"Drink it," he said. "It'll warm you up a little."

Rita wolfed down the food and drained the glass of strong Italian brandy out of a wine glass. When she was finished, Lovato said, "I'm going to walk you over to your room. Everything is the same as you left it. But the cops took your bag with the uniforms and shoes in it. I don't have to tell you what they found inside it."

"No," said Rita, "I don't know what they found."

"Come on," said Lovato, "who you trying to kid? Did your boyfriend get you tied up in some kind of drug mess at that resort?"

115

Rita's eyes pleaded with him to stop talking. Lovato took the hint, and said, "Okay, maybe I don't wanna know right now. Come on," he said, helping her up.

He led her out the kitchen door and up the stairs outside of the garage. He unlocked the door for her, and said, "You sleep. Don't leave the apartment until I tell you to. All of your clothes are here, and I'll leave some breakfast outside your door before I head to work in the morning. Make yourself scarce. We have a lot of talking to do."

Before going into her room, Rita put a hand on her cousin's cheek, and said, "Thank you, Richie. You are so good to me."

"Yeah, yeah," said Lovato.

He kissed her on the forehead, and said, "Sleep as late as you want. Just stay in your room, you hear me? We have someone taking care of Tommy
now. She don't know nothing, and I don't want her to know. I bring Marie to work with me in the morning, but I'll find a reason to leave lunchtime."

Rita said, "How's he doing?"

"About the same," said Lovato. "He'll be happy to see you, but not for a while, Rita. We need to talk. We need to figure out what to do with you."

Rita hung her head, and said, "I know."

"How did you get here?" asked Lovato. "I heard a car speeding off. Rocco?"

"Yeah," said Rita. "He's not that bad of a guy, Richie. He's like me, really. Got himself into trouble early and is having trouble finding his way out. I actually think we have a future."

Before she could continue, Lovato put a finger to her lips, and said, "Go to sleep. You may see things differently when you wake up. I'll do my best for you, but you gotta do what I say. And I'm saying to stay put until I tell you it's safe to come out."

Rita wasn't sure it would ever be safe to come out.

# CHAPTER 36

Clarice was expecting us and anxious to fill us in the next morning. She sent her parents off to breakfast moments before we arrived, and they promised to bring some food back for her. In the meantime, we weren't going to let her out of our sight.

There was only one chair in the room, so we clustered around Clarice on the king-sized bed. She took a breath before she began.

"Okay, you already know that I'm here to put Denny away for the assault in his car and the loss of my unborn child."

We all nodded, but Marsha circled her hand in an impatient gesture for Clarice to continue.

"Denny is going down the drain, and that's where he belongs. The bigger mystery is who attacked me on the path, robbed me, and left me in the woods unconscious."

We continued to look at her, and Marsha twirled her hand again.

I gave Marsha a look, and said, "Take your time, Clarice."

"So, we showed up yesterday, and Ariti comes to me with a sack of my stuff. He's not sure it's all there, but assumes I would know."

"Was it all there?" asked Susie.

"Well, you know we always count our tips at the end of the shift, so I knew exactly what was supposed to be there: $324.12."

"Wow! You had a good night," said Mary-Ann.

"Ariti gave me the best station that night," said Clarice.

When Clarice didn't keep speaking, we prodded her along.

"Didn't they take some jewelry from you?" I asked.

"Yes, my Citizen's watch. It was on a gold band. But that was also returned."

We all looked at each other.

How long did Ariti have your stuff, and why did it take him so long to return it to you?" Susie asked.

117

"That's just it," said Clarice. "Ariti told us he had just received the money and the watch from the police, so they clearly removed it from the crime scene. I don't know why the police didn't tell us about it until just now. They never did find my key, though."

I sat there stroking my chin like I had a beard. I was inclined to think highly of Ariti and thought he had our best interests at heart. But how well did I actually know him? I'd only met him a couple of months ago. He treated us with respect, got us to hustle, brought us to the bank once or twice a week, and sent us protection when Clarice got assaulted. Of course, some of that protection just got bumped off by the Mob, but still.

"Maybe he had it all along and never turned it over to the police," I said.

"Wouldn't that be easy enough to check out?" asked Clarice.

"Not if you have the police in your pocket," I said. "Ariti has been here forever. Who knows what kind of connections he has?"

"Very weird," said Clarice. "You have a very devious mind, Amy."

"I'm just trying to consider all angles," I said.

"Who's he trying to protect?" asked Marsha. "His sister, maybe?"

"You mean Denny's wife?" asked Clarice.

"She's one and the same," I said. "Maybe she's been here the same time as you more than once."

Just then, someone knocked on the door, and we all jumped.

"Who is it?" yelled Mary-Ann.

"Room service. I've got breakfast for four here."

Clarice's parents decided to provide sustenance for all of us, and we were grateful because we hadn't eaten yet, and it was going to be a long morning. We kept quiet while the room service waiter put covered dishes on every available surface, along with orange juice and coffee. Silverware wrapped in white cloth napkins was placed on top of the metal dish covers.

Clarice rummaged through her paper bag and pulled out a ten. She thanked the waiter and pressed the bill in his hand.

The waiter thanked her, and said, "Let us know if you need anything else. Room service is number 4 on your dial."

We claimed our plates after he left and did our best to eat with them in our laps. We made fast work of the scrambled eggs, hash brown

118

potatoes, and toast, and got back to talking over coffee and rugelach. I could just imagine the O'Hares saying, "What the hell is 'ruggelatch'?" It cracked me up a little.

I mentioned to Clarice, between bites, "You may want to put that bag in a safe place and not flash its contents to anybody. It's hard to know who to trust around here."

"You're right," said Clarice, "I need to be more careful."

We got back to the subject of Denny's wife and Ariti's sister.

Marsha said, "Gina knew that Denny was carrying on with a cocktail waitress, and probably not for the first time. Maybe Ariti told her it was you, Clarice, and he tipped her off to where you were staying."

Clarice thought about it for a moment, and said, "Ariti did ask me if I was feeling okay that night. I made it through without collapsing, but not by much. Maybe he sent Gina out to confront me. When Ariti told me to knock off early because I looked 'peaked,' I told him I was okay but would go straight back to the cabin after work."

We all exchanged ecstatic glances, like we solved a major puzzle. But our excitement was short-lived.

"Maybe she came out to confront me but got scared when I passed out. She couldn't have known I was injured and on the verge of miscarriage, could she? Maybe she panicked, dumped me in the woods, and took my money and watch to make it look like a mugging. Maybe she took my stuff and gave it to Ariti to put in his safe until they worked out a story."

"It *was* a mugging," said Marsha. "And you could have died out there in those woods."

"That's true," said Clarice. "But what's really crazy is the whole deal about my shoes. Why take my shoes and put them under my bed? Somebody clearly knew where I slept. Do you think that Sabra had something to do with this? Is there a connection there?"

"Well, there's definitely a connection between Sabra and Drew and Rita and Rocco," Susie said.

We all chewed on that for a while, when Marsha said, "Is there a connection between Ariti and those drug traffickers?"

119

"And is Gina actually his sister?" I asked. "Ariti couldn't have known that Clarice got punched by Denny that afternoon. Maybe Ariti is romantically involved with Gina and they set Denny up to take the fall for the attack on the path. Gina would have access to Denny's belongings. Maybe the law found something of his in the woods that would implicate him."

Clarice massaged her temples like she was developing a headache.

"Maybe we'll get some answers this afternoon," she said. "My parents
and I are meeting with the local authorities."

"Ah, yes," I said. "Possibly members of Ariti's extended family."

We polished off the rest of the rugelach and got up to leave, just as the O'Hares returned to the room.

# CHAPTER 37

As promised, Lovato came to Rita's door at lunchtime the next day. He carried a paper bag filled with Italian subs, chips, and two small Dr. Peppers. He noticed that the Danish and coffee he had left that morning was still on the welcome mat. That made him nervous.

"Open up, Rita," he said, knocking on the door. "It's Richie."

He was on the verge of using his key when he heard feet shuffling across the floor. Rita opened the door in a robe and gave her cousin a sleepy smile.

"How'd you sleep?" Lovato asked.

"Like I was dead," Rita said, sardonically.

"No joke," said Lovato, "because you coulda been."

"Don't I know it," said Rita.

Lovato followed her into the studio apartment and put the bag down on the drop-leaf table in the kitchenette. He went to the cupboard beside the small refrigerator and plucked out two plates.

"Sit down," he commanded, as he put the plates on the table. "Let's eat and talk. I have to get back to the store in an hour."

Rita sat down and unwrapped her sandwich while Lovato placed one of the bottles in front of her.

"You need a glass?" he asked.

"No," she said, taking a swig. "This'll do, thanks."

"So, you tell me your side, and I'll tell you mine," said Lovato.

Rita began, "I met Rocco at the steakhouse, when I was waitressing there. It was a slow night. We came on to each other a little, and he convinced me that I could make more money if I went to work at one of the resorts during high season. He told me he had a contact there, who ended up being my boss: George Ariti. It turns out that he and Ariti had other contacts in common, and not very savory ones."

Lovato looked like he wanted to say something but stopped himself with a mouthful of chips.

"Marty was going to come after me for the money I took from him out of desperation. I wanted him off my back so I could try to get on with my life without constantly looking over my shoulder, you know?

Lovato nodded and let her continue.

"You know I had a pretty troubled youth, and maybe that's an understatement. I'm not a kid anymore, and I didn't want to end up back in jail after so many clean years. But I didn't want to end up dead either. Rocco and I had chemistry from the start, and he had a way about him that made me want to help him."

Lovato couldn't control himself.

"Yeah, he's a conman," he interjected.

Rita nodded, and said, "And apparently, I'm not too smart."

"Damn right," said Lovato, with a smile. "Keep going."

"So, it turns out that Ariti isn't the only person he knows. He also knows Marty and God-knows-who-else because they're all, for lack of a better word, wise guys."

Lovato closed his eyes and shook his head slowly.

Rita took a sip of her Dr. Pepper, and continued.

"I tried to walk away, but he convinced me that if I did a small job for him, I could get myself off the hook with Marty and disappear. After a while, it sounded like he wanted me to disappear with *him*. He had his own debt to pay to some loan shark, and then he was going to go straight, and we could have a new start.

"Oh, brother," said Lovato, wiping his hands together instead of using a napkin. "And the kids who got killed?"

"Those kids weren't such kids," said Rita. "They were well into their twenties and had been involved in drug trafficking for years. Hoffman's was just one of their gigs. But they weren't brought in until after I left. Rocco was tasked with procuring heroin from people I didn't want to meet. And I was tasked with getting that heroin into the proper hands at Hoffman's and collecting money for it. I delivered that money to Rocco, and he gave me a cut. But most of my earnings went to Marty through Rocco."

"Are you sure?" asked Lovato.

"Why would he lie about that?" asked Rita. "Haven't you ever heard of honor among thieves?"

"Omerta?" said Lovato. "Yeah, I heard of that."

"Anyway," said Rita, "Rocco wanted me to do one more job after my two weeks were up to help him get out from under, but after Sabra and Drew got killed he decided it wasn't worth putting me in more danger. He says he loves me. And that's why he dropped me back here. Maybe he'll come back, or maybe he won't."

Lovato said, "You done?"

"Rita said, "Yeah."

"Eat your sub," he said. "I'm gonna talk now."

"Okay," she said, taking a bite.

"First of all," he started, "you're my cousin, and I love you. I don't want to see any harm come to you, but I have a wife and son to worry about. They're my number-one priority. I was literally left holding the bag when you disappeared, and that bag had heroin dust in it. I felt like a dope when they told me. Everyone, including the cops, knows that you were dealing drugs at Hoffman's. They're going to get you at some point, and, when they do, I don't want them pointing the finger at me. You understand? I'm a respectable businessman here. So, second of all, I'm not gonna go down for harboring a felon."

Rita flinched at the word.

"That's a little harsh, isn't it Richie?"

"Nah. It's the truth. But I'm gonna give you a little advice."

"Yeah?"

"Turn yourself in. Maybe they'll show you a little mercy. Tell them you got desperate because you were getting threatened by some bad guys. You don't gotta tell them it was Marty."

"Oh, believe me," said Rita, "if they force me to tell them it was Marty, I'll be dead for sure."

"Tell them you owed someone some money and feared for your life if you didn't return it. You were a hard-working waitress who took care of a sick nephew during the day and, all of a sudden, some grifter talked you into delivering drugs to get yourself outta debt. They know the Mob preys on the weak."

"Rocco himself told me to sell him out if I had to," admitted Rita.

"So, do it," said Rocco. "He's up shit's creek anyway."

"He may escape this whole mess," said Rita. "I think he might be heading to Canada."

"Border Patrol won't let him into Canada," said Lovato. "He's a wanted man now."

"For God's sake, Richie, it's not like he's killed anyone."

"How do you know?" he said. "He coulda set up a hit on those kids, for all you know."

Rita gave him a blank look. The sub sat mostly uneaten on her plate.

"Think about it, Rita. In a day or two, I'll be calling the cops myself. I gotta know one thing before I go. Whose hands were you putting that heroin into at Hoffman's?"

Rita looked Lovato in the eyes, and said, "George Ariti's.

After a moment, she added, "And Drew's hands. I put heroin into Drew's hands; the guy who got killed yesterday."

# CHAPTER 38

Clarice sat with her parents in a small conference room at the police station in Liberty. Her father drummed his fingers on the scarred oak table while her mother drank tepid coffee. Clarice studied her fingernails and wondered about what more she would learn that afternoon.

Clarice recognized the men that entered the room: Officer Ed Wiley and Officer Ryan Parker. They were the two officers who had found her in the woods. Parker smiled at her and her parents, but it was Wiley who addressed her.

"It's good to see you looking so well, Clarice," he said warmly. "Thank you for coming in today, and thank you, Mr. and Mrs. O'Hare, for being here with your daughter."

"We wouldn't miss it," said Clarice's father.

"It's good to see you, too, Officer Wiley," said Clarice.

Wiley pointed to a cassette player on the middle of the table, and said, "I would like to record today's conversation, with your permission, Clarice."

Clarice said, "Yes, that would be okay."

"Good," said Wiley, with a smile.

He turned on the cassette player, and said, "This is Officer Ed Wiley interviewing Clarice O'Hare regarding her two assaults on July 18, 1973; one in a vehicle owned and driven by Denny Martin on Rte. 17 near Monticello, New York, and one at Hoffman's Resort in the hamlet of Ferndale, New York, part of the Village of Liberty. Miss O'Hare and Mr. Martin were both employees of Hoffman's Resort on that date. We will be discussing Miss O'Hare's memory of the events, in addition to our own findings on the cases."

Wiley rewound the recording and played it back to check sound quality. Satisfied, he asked Clarice if she was ready to begin. She nodded her head.

Turning the cassette player back on, Wiley said, "A lot has happened since we last met, Clarice. First, I want you to know that Denny Martin will be serving time for assaulting you. We already have your statement about the battery that occurred in his vehicle that left you with grievous injuries that led to the loss of your unborn child. The doctors at Monticello Hospital will testify that the blows to your lower abdomen caused your miscarriage."

"We already knew that, Officer Wiley, said Clarice's father.

"I'm just getting started, Mr. O'Hare," said Wiley.

O'Hare settled back in his chair and looked at Wiley expectantly.

Wiley said to Clarice, "I assume you got your possessions back."

Clarice said, "Yes. Mr. Ariti returned them to me yesterday. I was wondering why we didn't hear about their discovery sooner."

Wiley meshed his fingers on the tabletop, and said, "This is an ongoing investigation. I have a few things to tell you, but mostly, I will be asking the questions. I would like you to tell me everything you recall from that day."

Clarice sat forward in her chair, and said, "We already went over that,"

"Time has passed since your attack," said Wiley. "You may remember more now."

Clarice settled back down, and recited, "I was out for a ride with Denny. I told him I thought I was pregnant, and maybe he would ask me to marry him. That's when he told me about his wife and two kids. I had no idea. I told him I wouldn't give the baby up. He punched me in the stomach twice, grabbed me by the face, and shoved me back against the car seat. He also warned me to keep my mouth shut."

Wiley sat nodding. "Did you pressure Mr. Martin in any way?"

Clarice thought for a moment, and said, "When he got nasty about me not considering an abortion, I may have told him I was going to tell his wife about us. I was angry, you know? I didn't want to be an unwed mother, but I'm Catholic and against abortion."

"I understand," said Wiley. "It sounds like he felt threatened by you."

126

Clarice reared back, and said, "You're not trying to make this *my* fault, are you?"

"I'm just trying to establish a motive for the attack."

"Yes, I threatened to expose him to his wife for lying to me about his marital status and making me pregnant," Clarice huffed.

Wiley said, "Denny is already going away for this attack, but we are exploring possible motives for a secondary attack."

"What do you mean?" asked Clarice. "Are you thinking that he's the one who assaulted me on the path and left me in the woods?"

"We have reason to believe that he was involved in the second assault, yes."

"What makes you think so?" asked Clarice. "Did you find some evidence at the scene?"

"We found a golf tee," said Wiley.

It sounded funny and Clarice started to chuckle. There were lots of golfers at Hoffman's.

"Tell me what else you remember," said Wiley.

"Well, it had been a grueling night. I was hurting all over and bleeding from what was probably the beginning of a miscarriage. I usually went out with the girls after work but I begged off that night. It wasn't exactly night, although it was still dark. We usually finished at 4 a.m. So, in addition to being hurt, I was on the verge of collapsing from exhaustion. Somebody grabbed me by the throat and also covered my mouth to keep me from screaming, I guess. I do remember smelling something sweet, and I realized, just today, that it was Rive Gauche."

"Would you please explain what that is, Clarice?"

"It's a popular perfume. I don't wear it but a lot of women do."

Satisfied, Wiley said, "Continue."

Clarice said, "I don't remember anything after that. I woke up in the woods, and that's when I saw you and your partner. She gestured at Parker, who was still smiling.

Wiley suddenly shut off the cassette player and considered the O'Hares for a moment. He asked Clarice, "Have you ever met Mr. Martin's wife, Gina?"

"Not that I'm aware of. If she ever visited the resort, he never pointed her out. He told me she occasionally came with their children, and they went elsewhere. Like, he mentioned the Amish country."

"Would it surprise you to know that his wife was visiting the night you got attacked on the path?" asked Wiley.

"Yes, it would surprise me," said Clarice. "Surely, Denny and I wouldn't have gone out for that afternoon drive if his wife was around."

Wiley said, "I didn't say she was there that afternoon. She came down that evening, after work. She left the kids at home with their nanny. Mr. Martin says he had invited her up to try to make amends. He wanted her there alone so he could explain things and maybe get absolution."

"So, you think he was planning to break up with me before I announced my pregnancy?" asked Clarice. "Do you think he pointed me out to his wife in the dining room?"

"Not necessarily," said Wiley. "Did you know that Gina is George Ariti's sister?"

"I didn't know that until yesterday, when one of the other cocktail waitresses told me," said Clarice.

"Which one would that be?" asked Wiley.

"Susie, but I don't want to get her involved in this."

"It'll be between us," said Wiley.

"I also learned that Gina is currently staying at Hoffman's with her children."

"Who told you that?" asked Wiley.

"Amy. They met by accident at the lake, and they started a conversation."

Clarice's father interrupted, "Do you have a suspect in my daughter's assault, or just a bunch of suspicions and a golf tee?"

Wiley turned to face O'Hare, and said, "We have two confessions. The Martins were the last to leave the cocktail lounge that night, and they were both pretty drunk. When they left the hotel, they spotted Clarice on the path. Mr. Martin tried to keep his wife from confronting your daughter, but she was out of control and grabbed Clarice from behind. Clarice went down easily. She was very weak. Mr. Martin could have carried Clarice into the cabin — he found her key — but he was very intoxicated, and it was

128

easier for him to just deposit her in the woods next to the path. Gina noticed Clarice's shoes, and asked her husband, 'What should we do with these?' Mr. Martin gave her the key to the cabin and told her exactly where to leave them. Before putting the shoes under Clarice's bed, Gina scattered Clarice's money and watch to passively add insult to injury. You know, "Hell hath no fury, etc."

O'Hare asked, "If the Martins confessed to Clarice's assault, why are you interrogating my daughter? And why did Mr. Ariti have my daughter's possessions?"

Wiley said, "Mr. Ariti doesn't care what happens to Denny Martin. We're already dealing with him. But he does care about what happens to his sister. It was Gina who led us to you later that morning, Clarice. She had already gathered your belongings and given them to her brother for safekeeping. Denny is willing to take responsibility for the whole attack because he wants to see his kids again, and Gina told him he won't if he implicates her in any way, even if it's the truth."

"So, what do you want from my daughter?" asked O'Hare.

"Mr. Ariti is a very important man in these parts, Mr. O'Hare. He's a major philanthropist, and has made generous donations to all sorts of causes in our community. We wouldn't cover up a crime for him, but if we can do something for him that doesn't impact negatively on anybody, we do. Now that you know what happened on that path, and why, he would like you to forget about Gina's part and not press charges against her. In fact, she came up here to apologize to you in person. In private, of course. You would have to sign a piece of paper exonerating her from blame. And Mr. Ariti would be much obliged. He would make it worth your while. And, believe me, you want a guy like Mr. Ariti on your side. You want him owing you; not the other way around."

O'Hare said, "You want my daughter to perjure herself?"

"Nothing of the kind," Wiley said. "All she needs to do is say she doesn't remember anything other than the scent of perfume before fainting. And frankly, that perfume could have rubbed off on Denny Martin long before he and his wife headed down that path."

O'Hare said, "We'll think about it, but things don't happen like this in Texas." Wiley said, "You're a long way from Texas, Mr. O'Hare."

# CHAPTER 39

Rita had to come up with a plan, and fast. Her cousin's hospitality wasn't going to last long and for good reason. Lovato gave his son's caretaker a day off so Rita could have a little more time with her nephew. Lovato's wife didn't think that was too great an idea, but she allowed it when her husband promised her that Rita would be gone in a day or two, tops. Nobody had any idea of what "gone" meant.

Rita mulled her options. As Lovato had suggested, she could turn herself into the police, but that would probably lead to another stint in prison. Because she was a repeat offender, it was possible she'd go away for a long time, in the prime of her life. The thought of that didn't appeal to her.

She still had some money on her. She could move out of Lovato's garage and find herself a room somewhere, and pay cash. That might buy her a little time. She even considered getting her old job back at the steakhouse. Maybe Rocco would find her there.

Rita didn't know how to get in touch with Rocco. How was she supposed to tell him where she was? She didn't even know if he was dead or alive at that moment.

Then, she thought about George Ariti. She knew it was he who had sent the champagne to her and Rocco at the end of her job at Hoffman's. The card had said, "I owe you." She still had it. How did she know it was Ariti who'd sent the card? Because she had heard those words directly from his lips on the day they met.

Rocco had arranged that meeting.

When Rita came to work that first night, she was taken directly to Ariti's office by a hostess. The hostess said, "Just knock, he's expecting you."

Rita was left alone in the quiet hallway. She wondered if she should run. She knew that this job would put her back in the criminal realm, but not for long. Rocco had promised her that she would be in and out in two weeks. She thought about getting Marty off her back, and that made it easier to take the next step. She took a deep breath and rapped gently on the door. Ariti answered immediately. He extended a hand and ushered her into his lugubrious office.

"Welcome, Rita," he said.

Rita noted that Ariti was a handsome man with olive skin, black wavy hair, and impenetrable eyes. She guessed him to be in his late-forties, but he could have been older. He had a sad face that communicated kindness and paternal concern, but it was not made for smiling.

Rita said, "Thank you, Mr. Ariti."

Ariti showed her to a chair and told her to be seated. Rita looked around the office and saw only darkness there: shades drawn, mahogany furniture, burgundy couch, mud-colored walls. The chair she sat in enveloped her in upholstered murk. Rita wondered if Ariti would go up in flames if he went out after sunrise.

The room was forbidding, but Ariti was warm.

"It's *I* who should be thanking *you*," he said. "This is not a job for just anybody. Rocco chose you very carefully, and I have always found him to be very trustworthy."

Rita wasn't sure if she should say anything. She wanted to ask how Ariti and Rocco knew each other but she sensed it was not the time to be chatty. Besides, she wasn't born yesterday. She assumed they were part of the same "family."

"Can you keep a secret, Rita?" asked Ariti.

For a moment, Rita considered saying, "No," and bolting out of the room, but she nodded instead.

She said, "Rocco has already informed me of the delicate nature of this job."

"Good," said Ariti. "And you are clear about your role in it?"

"Yes, I am clear," she said.

Ariti came out from behind his desk and walked toward Rita. She braced herself but didn't know what for. Ariti reached out with both hands and adjusted the wig on her head.

"I wanted to meet you before sending you out on your first mission," he said. "Tonight, I want you to just wait tables, like the other girls. They will show you the ropes. They're likely to be curious about you. Be friendly, but keep to yourself. They will wonder why you don't sleep in the cabin with them. You can tell them you have a boyfriend to go home to. Don't let them see you without your wig on."

"Doesn't it look obvious?" asked Rita.

"Only if you don't wear it right," he said.

Rita didn't say anything, so Ariti continued, "Your driver will provide you with product. You will bring that product with you in the afternoon and leave it in my safe. After work, you will come back to my office, remove your wig, change back into street clothes, and deliver the product to a party I will identify. That party will have an envelope full of cash for you. You will take that envelope and give it to your driver, and he will take over from there. Over the next two weeks, you will take this action four times. Your cut will be five percent after we total everything up two weeks from now. That's when you will go missing, and a replacement will be brought in."

"Won't people wonder where I am?" asked Rita.

"People come and go around here," said Ariti.

"So, I do my two weeks and I'm done?" asked Rita.

"Yes, my usual girl is coming back. Listen, the less you know, the better. I told Rocco I needed someone for a couple of weeks, and he told me you'd be perfect for the job. That's all the credentials I need. That, and your ability to keep this all confidential. If you do your part well, I'll owe you."

His face creased into an attempt at a grin.

"Rita smiled back, and said, "I'll do my best, Mr. Ariti."

132

# CHAPTER 40

By the time Clarice got back to the room with her mother and father, the girls were out doing their afternoon activities. She could have tried to find them at the lake, but the girls had given her strict instructions to stay hidden with her parents. Her friends didn't know what she now knew, that both Denny and his wife were involved in her attack that night in July. According to Wiley, Gina was drunk and upset at the time but was now seeking Clarice's pardon. Clarice wasn't enthusiastic about meeting her, but she was no longer fearful about it. This was going to have to be kept a secret.

Clarice stayed in the room watching TV with her parents until she heard familiar voices outside the door. She jumped up and opened it before anyone had a chance to knock. The girls nearly tumbled into the room. Clarice's parents offered to leave, and nobody stopped them. Clarice caught a warning glance from her father on his way out. As soon as they were gone, the girls surrounded Clarice on the bed again.

"Tell us everything," said Susie. "Leave nothing out."

Clarice wasn't a skilled liar, but she had discussed the situation with her parents on the way back from the police station. Even her mother spoke. They told her to keep it simple and include the truth. They didn't care if Denny took the entire fall for Clarice's troubles. And it sounded like George Ariti was willing to make a grand gesture to keep Clarice silent about Gina, like pay her college tuition. Then, they could get out of here and put it all behind them – after they met with Ariti and Gina.

"Denny was the only culprit," said Clarice. "Apparently, he wasn't satisfied with just working me over in his car. His wife came up that night and, as you already know, Gina is Ariti's sister. Ariti told Gina that Denny was cheating on her again after swearing he wouldn't do it anymore. That was after Denny told Gina he wanted to make amends. She called him a lying, cheating bastard. And she told him she was filing for divorce and that he could forget about seeing his children again. They had a big fight and, when she stormed off in the middle of the night, he got drunk and laid in wait for me. He knew when I got off work. When he saw me part ways with you, he followed me down the path, made sure that nobody was around, and grabbed me by the throat. He got scared when I went down so quickly, and dragged me into the woods. He scattered my belongings out of spite and left. But that's when he saw my shoes on the path. He had my key, so he let himself into the cabin and put them under my bed to make it look like I'd been there. A security guard found me later that morning and alerted the police. The police found Denny sleeping it off in his cottage the next morning. They brought him to the station, and he confessed."

Before Clarice could continue, Susie asked, "So, what became of Denny? And why didn't the police tell you about this sooner? Is he in custody, or what?"

Clarice's mind went blank. She hadn't anticipated these questions. She had no idea where Denny was, and hadn't thought to ask. One thing she did know: She never wanted to see him again.

"They told me he was going away, but they didn't say where, and I didn't ask," she said. "I don't know why they didn't tell me sooner. You know police – they need to go through evidence and all that stuff. As for the third question, I believe he is in custody."

I said, "You believe, but you're not certain?"

"I'm not certain," Clarice said, "but it was implied that he was in custody. It's not going to matter much to me. My parents are taking me home tomorrow, and I won't be coming back."

That's when Clarice slipped up.

"Ariti wants my parents and me to have dinner with him and Gina tonight."

"Really?" said Marsha. "Here?"

"No, he's taking us to a restaurant in town."

"What for?" Marsha persisted. "And why with Gina?"

Clarice felt flustered but fought for calm.

"I guess he wants to make sure I have a sense of closure in all this," said Clarice. "Maybe Gina needs to have that, too. After all, it sounds like I was the straw that broke the camel's back when it came to her marriage. I wasn't the first woman that Denny had cheated on her with, but I was certainly the last. Ariti knows that Denny wronged us both. I think he wants to put all this to rest."

We all nodded our heads in acceptance, until Mary-Ann spoke up.

"Do you think the police took care of Denny, or do you think Ariti took care of Denny?"

"What are you talking about?" Clarice asked. "You think that Ariti made Denny disappear?"

"I wouldn't rule it out," said Mary-Ann. "There's something screwy going on around here. And I'm wondering if Drew and Sabra had anything to do with it."

"What about Drew and Sabra?" asked Clarice.

"Oh, my God," said Marsha. "Nobody told you about Drew and Sabra? They're both dead."

"What?" squealed Clarice.

"Yeah, they got shot just a few days ago, gangland-style," said Marsha, making a shooting gesture with her fingers. "There's a lot of Mob activity going on around here."

"Jesus!" said Clarice. "I can't wait to get out of here."

"Be careful when you go out with Ariti and his sister tonight," I said. "I'm starting to feel like he might be connected, if you know what I mean."

Clarice went pale.

"And I'm guessing that Drew was the security guard who found you in the woods," I said.

# CHAPTER 41

Lovato drove Rita to a phone booth in downtown Ellenville and asked her if she needed any change. She told him she had plenty and got out of the car. Lovato watched her enter the booth and close the glass door behind her. For twenty cents, an operator would connect her with Hoffman's. It was late afternoon, and she knew that Ariti would be there. At least, that was when he always met with her in his gloomy office.

Rita connected with a Hoffman's operator, who told her to please hold for Mr. Ariti. Rita nearly froze when she heard Ariti's voice. She didn't know how to begin. Finally, she spoke.

"Hello, Mr. Ariti. This is Rita Connelly, Rocco's friend."

"Well, hello, Rita," he responded. "It's good to hear your voice. How are you?"

Rita decided to spill the beans. She was exhausted and didn't know where to turn. Ariti was her only hope.

"Not too good, Mr. Ariti," she said, trying to hold back tears. "I'm sure you heard what happened to Sabra and Drew."

Ariti cleared his throat, and said, "Where are you calling from, Rita?"

"Don't worry, Mr. Ariti," she said. "I'm calling from a payphone. Nobody knows I'm here except for my cousin. You met him. Richard Lovato, remember?"

"Yes, I remember Mr. Lovato," said Ariti. "And I'm well aware of what happened to Sabra and Drew. What a tragedy. What can I do for you, my dear?"

Rita tried to calm herself but her heart was racing. She hoped the operator wasn't listening in. To be on the safe side, she put an extra sixty cents into the coin slot.

"I'm scared, Mr. Ariti," she said in a loud whisper. "After Sabra and Drew got murdered on the highway, Rocco didn't want to put me at any more risk. He dropped me off at my cousin's house a couple of nights ago, but I can't stay with him anymore. He has his own family to think about. He's been very kind to me. I can't put him or his family in danger. But I don't know where to go next, Mr. Ariti. I don't even feel safe in this phone booth."

Ariti considered for a moment, and said, "I'm going to send a driver to pick you up. You remember Joe, don't you? Tell me exactly where you are. He'll come for you."

"Oh, thank you, Mr. Ariti," said Rita, feeling relieved.

She told Ariti that the phone booth was on Canal Street, in front of a Woolworth's.

"Should I wait in the car with my cousin?" she asked

"No," said Ariti. "Send your cousin home and stay in the booth as long as you can. If someone is desperate to use it, just get out and stand near the entrance to Woolworth's. Joe is on his way. Don't worry, honey. We'll take care of you."

"Thanks a million, Mr. Ariti. But there's one more thing. Have you heard from Rocco?"

"Let's talk about that when I see you," he said, and hung up.

Rita left the booth to speak with Lovato.

"Didja reach him?" he asked, looking up at her through the partially rolled-down passenger window.

"Yes, I did," said Rita. "He's sending someone to pick me up."

"Where they taking you?" he asked.

"I don't know yet," she said. "But the driver should be here soon, and Mr. Ariti wanted me to send you away."

Rita looked nervously at the phone booth, afraid that someone would take her place. She wanted the protection of those glass doors.

"For the record," said Lovato, "I still think you should turn yourself in to the police. You're lying down with criminals, Rita. I don't see this ending too good."

"I'll be okay, Richie, don't worry," said Rita. "I'll call you when I get settled. Why would anyone want to harm me?"

"Collateral damage, maybe? You never know with these guys. I've been trying to steer clear of them my whole life, seems like."

"You never did get over your stint in Korea, Richie."

"I'm not talking about Korea," said Lovato. "I'm talking about what's going on in our streets right here."

"I feel confident that Mr. Ariti will take care of me. But you've got to go now, Richie. Please go. I'll be all right. I love you, Richie."

"I love you, too, Rita. Take care of yourself. And let me know you're okay."

"I will," said Rita. "I promise, I will."

Lovato turned on the car and pulled away from the curb. Rita didn't return to the phone booth until she saw his vehicle make a turn on the next block. Then, she sat on the fold-down seat and closed the glass door before picking up the receiver and pretending to have a conversation. The street wasn't busy and nobody disturbed her.

Rita was expecting a red Mustang but the car that pulled up to the curb outside of Woolworth's was a blue Pinto. And she didn't see Lovato's car turn back onto Canal Street several cars behind it.

# CHAPTER 42

Clarice and her parents waited in front of the hotel for their pickup. Mrs. O'Hare noted that there was a chill in the air as she buttoned up her pink cardigan.

She said, "Do you have any idea where we're going, Clarice?"

"No, Mama, I sure don't," said Clarice. "The only place I know of around here is the Mountaintop, and I can't believe we'll be going there, especially not in a limo."

"Isn't that the restaurant down the hill from here?" asked Mr. O'Hare.

"Yes, Daddy."

"Sounds kind of funny, calling a downhill place the "Mountaintop."

They all agreed on that and shared a chuckle.

A long black car pulled up and the driver, who didn't look like a chauffeur, rolled down his darkened window, and asked, "Are you the O'Hares?"

Mr. O'Hare said, "Yes."

The driver got out of the car and opened the back door. This was a limo intended to carry six people. The O'Hares sat next to each other, all opting to face forward.

"Can you tell me where we're going?" asked Mr. O'Hare.

"I'm taking you to dinner with Mr. Ariti," the driver said. "Sit back, and enjoy the ride. We'll be there in about fifteen minutes. Would you like to hear some music?"

"For a moment, Mr. O'Hare wondered if the driver could find some Waylon Jennings way up here in New York State, but decided not to ask.

"No, thank you," he said.

In late August, there was still plenty of daylight left, even at 7:30 p.m. The O'Hares wordlessly watched the scenery roll by until the limo suddenly turned onto a dirt road and proceeded into the lush forest.

"Is this some kind of shortcut?" asked Mr. O'Hare.

"No, sir," said the driver. "This is the most direct route to dinner. I am taking you to Mr. Ariti's private residence."

The O'Hares were hoping for a more public setting, in case they needed to yell for help. But there was no turning back now. Mrs. O'Hare reached for her husband's hand.

After bumping along for several minutes, they came to a clearing with an attractive log house in front of them. The curtains were drawn, and it looked uninhabited.

"Is Mr. Ariti actually here?" asked Mr. O'Hare.

"Oh, yes, he's here. His car is parked out back."

Just then, Ariti came to greet them at the door. It was the first and only time Clarice had ever seen him out of a suit. Somehow, he still managed to look formal in khaki pants, a dark-green pullover, and brown loafers. He held out a hand and welcomed them in to a large rustic living room. Clarice was half-expecting to see a buck head over the fireplace, but there was large painting instead. It looked like a Modigliani.

Ariti gestured to a leather couch and asked them to have a seat. He took one of the flowery upholstered chairs opposite.

"Gina will be with us in a minute," he said. "She's in the kitchen, fixing hors d'oeuvres."

"Thank you for having us to your beautiful home, Mr. Ariti," said Mrs. O'Hare. "So gracious of you."

"We would have brought something if we knew we were coming to your house," said Mr. O'Hare.

"Oh, no worries. How were you to know? It's just that the restaurants around here are packed at the end of summer, and I wanted us to be able to talk in peace. We've had some serious business between us, haven't we?"

"Yes, we have," admitted Mr. O'Hare.

Clarice sat quietly surveilling the room. She was not looking forward to meeting Denny's wife and wanted the evening to end as quickly as possible.

"How about a drink?" asked Ariti. "I'm taking orders."

There was a wet bar in the living room. Ariti went behind it, fixed beverages, and delivered them on a silver tray, not at all like the cork-and-plastic trays that were used at Hoffman's. As he was doling out drinks, a dark, slender woman entered the room carrying canapés on a big round plate.

"There she is," said Ariti. "Allow me to introduce my sister, Gina."

Gina gave everyone a smile, and said, "Hello."

Mr. O'Hare got up to shake her hand. His wife and daughter remained seated.

Gina said, "Thank you so much for agreeing to meet with us, especially you, Clarice."

Clarice nodded, but said nothing.

Gina sat in one of the flowery chairs, and said, "I want to get everything out in the open and apologize for any wrongdoing on my part."

Clarice continued to watch her. She thought that Gina and Ariti were probably half-siblings because they looked at least fifteen years apart in age. On the other hand, they both had the same beautiful black wavy hair and slender body build.

Gina continued, "As you surely know by now, my husband and I have been having marital problems for a long time. Denny has been cheating on me with one woman after another for years."

Clarice said, "Go on."

Gina bent closer to Clarice, and continued.

"I was pretty young when we got married. I'd met him at Hoffman's when I came to visit my brother one summer. We dated for a long time before we got married, and the kids came a few years later. I had my work in Westchester County and he had his work here, at least during the summer. During the winter, he was mostly home with me and the children. But during the summer, all rules went out the window. He cheated on me relentlessly, even brazenly. I was humiliated."

Clarice said, "I understand, and I am sorry I was one of those young women he cheated on you with. He presented himself to me as single, and I was too naïve to question it."

Gina said, "It is so not your fault, Clarice."

Clarice nodded.

"But this is the first time I ever heard about him attacking someone. George told me about what happened to you and how you landed in the hospital."

"He damaged my little girl," said O'Hare. "She may never be able to have children, thanks to your husband."

Nobody had reached for a canapé, but everyone had a sip from their glasses.

"I can't tell you how sorry I am," said Gina. "If it's any consolation to you, Denny won't be having any more children either."

"What's done is done, Gina," said Clarice. "His loss doesn't make me any more able to have children."

Gina hung her head, and said, "He will get his just desserts, and George and I will do whatever we can for you."

"What's your view on what happened on the path that night?" asked Clarice.

"Denny invited me to come to the hotel for a weekend, and make up. We went over to the cocktail lounge late and got roaring drunk. I'm surprised you didn't notice us."

"I mostly worked the dining room and nightclub that night," said Clarice. "But I'm surprised the other girls didn't say anything."

"Do you remember who was working the cocktail lounge after 2 a.m.?" asked Ariti."

Clarice thought for a moment, and said, "No, I don't."

"It was Sabra," said Ariti.

Clarice's eyes widened. She took a sip of Chablis, and said, "And now, she's dead."

The O'Hares grabbed for the canapés, and shoved them in their mouths.

"Yes," said Ariti, looking sadly into Clarice's eyes.

"Anyway," Gina continued, "Denny spotted you on the path when we left the cocktail lounge, and he said, 'Hey, there's Clarice.' When I asked him who Clarice was, he told me, and I took off after you, and he came after me. He outran me and grabbed you before I could even open my mouth. When you went down, I got scared and ran back to the hotel.

Denny did the rest. And, considering what he had done to you earlier, it's a miracle he didn't do more. Again, I am so sorry."

Clarice looked at Gina steadily, and said, "You remember a lot for someone who was dead drunk. How do you know what Denny did?"

"Because he told me, but not right away," said Gina. "On that night, I went back to the hotel and slept there. Denny managed to make it home afterwards, and he apparently passed out. He got awakened by the police the next morning, after a security guard found you in the woods."

"So, where's Denny now?" Clarice's father asked. "The police weren't too forthcoming about that, but they led us to believe he's in custody."

Without answering, Ariti suddenly got up, and said, "Why don't we all take a little stroll before dinner? I'd like to show you around before the sun goes down."

The O'Hares were taken aback by what seemed like an act of evasion on Ariti's part, but they all got up and followed him through the house to the back door. As they exited the house, they saw the limo driver sitting in an Adirondack chair on the back deck.

"Hey, Joe," said Ariti. "Are you ready for the grand tour?"

Joe said, "Yes, boss."

Joe got up and beckoned Clarice and her parents to follow him. Ariti and Gina brought up the rear. Clarice held her mother under the arm to keep her from falling in the woods and also to try to calm herself down. She wondered if they were being led to their death.

"We're not dressed for a hike," said Mr. O'Hare.

"Oh, no worries," said Joe, "we're not going very far."

The party approached a small outbuilding within a hundred yards of the house. It was surrounded by a copse of eastern hemlock that nearly blocked the short steps leading to its front door. Clarice noticed a small window near its pitched roof.

Joe walked up the steps and unlocked the door. He turned and beckoned the rest to follow, but the O'Hares stood in place, paralyzed with fear.

Mr. O'Hare turned to Ariti, and said, "We don't want any trouble, Mr. Ariti."

Ariti said, "Oh, please, Mr. O'Hare, I don't mean your family any harm. Back at the house, you were asking about Denny. I am merely answering your question, but this has got to be our little secret."

Clarice said, "I don't want to go in there, Daddy."

O'Hare said, "I don't want my wife and daughter exposed to any unpleasantness. If Denny is in your custody, I'm okay with that. Do whatever you want with him."

Ariti said, "Denny is in my custody, yes. I would like you to go into that shed with Clarice and hear him out before we deal with him. Your wife can wait out here with Gina."

Mr. O'Hare thought for a moment, and said, "Let me go in first. I don't want my daughter to see anything that will upset her further."

Ariti said, "As you wish."

Joe pushed the door open. Denny was sitting in a straight-backed chair in the middle of the room. He was bound and gagged and his hair was disheveled, but he seemed intact. Joe removed the gag and Denny immediately sputtered, "I know you're Clarice's father. George told me you were coming. I'm sorry for everything. Please tell Clarice I'm sorry for all I put her through. I've screwed up my whole life, I know that. But please accept my apology. Is she here? Can I see her? Please, let me see her. Let me apologize to her in person."

Before he could continue, Joe pushed the gag back into Denny's mouth.

Ariti asked, "Do you want to take a shot at him, Mr. O'Hare?"

O'Hare said, "You mean take a swing at him? No, I don't want his blood on my hands. I'm taking my daughter home tomorrow, and we don't ever want to see this man again."

Ariti said, "Don't worry, you won't. But remember our agreement. You say nothing about Denny to anyone, and your daughter gets a college education on me. I'm an honorable man, Mr. O'Hare, even if I seem like a bad guy. You might say some of us have a different code of ethics."

"I appreciate that, Mr. Ariti. But I'd like to get my wife and daughter safely home. Your secret is safe with us."

Ariti said, "Good," and he ushered O'Hare out of the shed.

"I will drive you and your family back to the hotel. Dinner is waiting for you in your room."

"What about Denny?" asked O'Hare.

"Don't worry about Denny. Joe will take him for a ride in the limo tomorrow. Tonight, he'll get to spend some time with Gina."

After he got the O'Hares seated in the back seat of his car, Ariti took Gina by the arm and led her a distance away.

"Thank you for your assistance, consigliere," he said, and kissed her on the cheek.

# CHAPTER 43

Rita approached the Pinto with trepidation. The last time she had seen it was a few days before, when Rocco had dropped her off near her cousin's house. When Ariti said he would send a driver, she expected to see Joe behind the wheel. She was surprised to see Rocco in the driver's seat, with his hair completely hidden under a Rastafarian hat and his eyes covered by dark shades.

"Ya, mon," she said, laughing. "I'm surprised you're not wearing a Bozo wig."

"Who says I'm not?" he said, laughing with her.

"I am so happy to see you," Rita said, reaching for his hand. "Has the danger passed? Where are we going? Are we safe in this car?"

"This car has plates from Vermont now, and there are lots of blue Pintos on the road," said Rocco.

"That's a relief. But we're not going to blow up, are we?" asked Rita.

"Whaddya talking about?"

"You haven't heard about the recall? These cars have bad fuel tanks in the back. Don't you read the papers?"

"Who has the time?" asked Rocco.

"Just don't get rear-ended," said Rita.

"Shit, this ain't even my car," said Rocco.

"Yeah," said Rita. "I would have preferred the Mustang."

"We're trying to keep a low profile here, Rita."

Rita shifted in her seat, and asked, "So, what's the plan?"

Rocco said, "I'm taking you to Ariti's house in the woods. We can hole up there for a few days, and then he's gonna try to get us out of the country."

Rita gave Rocco a long look, and asked, "Did you already complete your second job and pay off the sharks?"

Rocco turned away, and said, "Let's just say I did one and not the other."

Rita continued to looked at Rocco, and shouted, "For Christ's sake, are you trying to get us killed? Richie told me to turn myself in, and that's what I should have done."

Rocco hunched up his shoulders, and said, "Come on, Rita, give me a little credit. I'm gonna turn my earnings over to Ariti, and he's going to pay off the sharks. In exchange for the rest of the haul, he's going to get us the papers to get us out of the country."

"Where's he sending us, Rocco? Iceland?"

"Nah. What the hell would I do in Iceland? I'm no skater."

Rita turned to look out the passenger window. Her life began to pass before her eyes, and she suspected that she didn't have much time left. How could she possibly have gotten involved with another career criminal? Did she have that much of a death wish? She sat shaking her head. She thought about jumping out of the moving car.

Rocco reached out and touched her shoulder.

"Come on, baby, we'll be all right. I've done a lot of good work for Ariti over the years. He's an honorable man, underneath, like me. He got no bones with either of us."

Rita thought about how Ariti had treated her when she first came to his office. He was soft-spoken and compassionate. He looked her in the eyes. He connected with her. He made sure she understood what was expected of her. He reassured her of her safety. She felt his sincerity, his innate kindness. She was being asked to traffic heroin, and yet, he made her feel like she was on some saintly mission.

And here she was with Rocco. She loved him in spite of all he was and wasn't. He was doing his best to protect her, with his disguise and bogus license plate and potentially dangerous car. He was taking her into the woods to what he thought was a safe house. Rita suspected that Ariti was planning to kill them both, because why keep them around? It seemed to her that she and Rocco were liabilities, but what did she know of the true nature of their relationship?

Rocco pulled onto a dirt road and fishtailed his way through the woods.

"Please slow down," said Rita. "I'm in no hurry to get to wherever we're going."

"We're almost there," said Rocco, looking at her.

Rita suddenly yelled, "Keep your eyes on the road!"

They nearly collided with a black limo making its way down the rutted path. Rita recognized the driver behind the wheel. If anyone else was in the vehicle, Rita couldn't see them behind the darkened windows. Rocco pulled as far over as he could to let the other car pass. Joe acknowledged them with a salute as he continued driving, with trees reaching out to scratch his doors.

"What's a limo doing out here in the woods?" asked Rita.

"Leaving," said Rocco, mournfully.

# CHAPTER 44

The girls decided to pass on the Mountaintop after another long night of peddling whiskey and seltzer. They quietly went past Clarice's room a little after 4 a.m. and listened in at the door. If anyone was snoring in there, they didn't hear it.

"I feel tempted to knock," whispered Marsha.

"No, don't do that," I said. "Let them sleep. Who knows what kind of night they had."

"I wish I knew they were in there," Marsha persisted.

"Let it be, for now," I said. "We'll see her before she leaves later today. And, if we don't see her, then we'll have to do something about it."

Susie opened the door to our room and turned on the overhead light. She was the first to spot a piece of folded hotel stationary on the harvest gold rug. We nearly bumped into her as she bent over to retrieve it.

"What does it say?" asked Mary-Ann, before Susie had had a chance to even straighten up.

Susie walked into the room and turned on the nearest table lamp. Unfolding the note, she read, "Pleasant evening. Nothing much to report. Gina apologized and we parted okay. We're leaving earlier than expected in the morning so, if I don't see you, it was wonderful getting to know you all. I will be in touch." It was signed, "Clarice."

"What the hell?" said Marsha. "We're not even going to get to say good-bye? What's their hurry?"

"Sounds a little fishy to me," I said. "Maybe we should take turns sitting outside the room until they open their door to leave."

"I say we just knock on the door now," said Susie. "Clarice will understand."

The minute Susie stepped out of our room, Clarice opened the door to hers a crack and slipped out into the hall in her nightgown.

"You're here!" said Susie a little too loudly, and we all came tumbling after.

"Shhh," Clarice said, holding her forefinger to her lips. "You'll wake my parents."

We hustled Clarice into our room and shut the door softly. We all plopped down on one of the beds and began the interrogation.

"We got concerned when we saw your note just now," said Mary-Ann.

"I understand but I'm fine, as you can see," said Clarice.

"What time did you get back here?" I asked.

"About 9 p.m., I think," said Clarice, vaguely.

"So how was it?" asked Marsha. "Where'd you go?"

Clarice contemplated coming up with a fairy story but she already had too many other tales to keep track of. She didn't see any harm in telling them a small truth.

"Believe it or not, we went to Ariti's house. He said it was because the restaurants are so crowded at this time of year."

That made sense.

"No kidding," said Mary-Ann. "He cooked?"

"No, his sister cooked while he played bartender."

"What did you have?" asked Mary-Ann.

Oh, the details!

Clarice tried to remember the contents of the canapés, and came out with "Something with fish and avocados and cucumber. Very light and refreshing. No capon and kasha, but good."

She smiled.

"Was Ariti wearing a suit?" asked Marsha.

"No, he was casually but impeccably dressed. I didn't take him for a loafer guy, but he was."

"What did you think of Gina?" asked Marsha.

"She was nice enough," said Clarice. "Maybe a little cool. Slim and dark like Ariti. A lot younger than Denny, but a lot older than us. She's around Rita's age."

"Speaking of Gina, I said, "let's cut to the chase. What happened with her on the night you were attacked?"

Clarise could be truthful about that, too.

"She told me that she was out with Denny late that night," she said. They were in the cocktail lounge, getting drunk. They were there between 2 and 4 a.m. Sabra was working the lounge at that hour. Did any of you see them?"

None of us had, and we told that to Clarice. But we had gone out to the Mountaintop with Sabra after work, and she hadn't mentioned anything about seeing Denny and Gina. And now, she was dead.

"So, Gina apologized?" I asked.

"Yes," said Clarice, "she was very apologetic. It sounded like she had a history of being victimized by Denny, too."

"Well, you're both well rid of him," I said. "Does anyone know where he is?"

Clarice was able to answer that question truthfully, also. She knew where he was a few hours ago, but she had no idea of where he was now. He was supposedly leaving with the limo driver after she and her parents left with Ariti, but she didn't divulge that to us. Denny was probably sleeping with the fishes, if the Hudson River actually had fish in it.

"I'm guessing in custody," she said. "I don't know where."

We all accepted that and figured it was okay with us, as long as Clarice was out of danger and Denny was history. We would all be leaving soon to go on with our respective lives, and all of this would be a memory.

"Your note said you were leaving earlier than expected," said Susie.

"That's right," said Clarice. "My father really wants to get out of here. We have a flight out of Stewart International Airport at 1 p.m. It's about forty minutes from here, so we have a limo coming to pick us up at 10:30 this morning. Ariti arranged it for us. We could have flown directly from the hotel airport but my father wanted a direct flight to Dallas. We should probably say our good-byes now, so we can all get a little sleep."

We all hugged in the middle of the room, wishing her well, and telling her to keep in touch. We knew she was heading back to her sophomore year at Southern Methodist University, and I personally hoped she would never realize her bizarre premonition of dying in a fiery car crash. I hoped she would find a good man and manage to have children and a career. We never spoke about what she was majoring in or what she

151

wanted to do with her life, but now was not the time. We walked her to the door and kept it open until she was safely back in her own room.

When Clarice left us, we believed we had closed out one big chapter of our summer in the Catskills. Clarice hadn't been with us for very long, but we were going to remember her for a long time to come.

We were all awake and having breakfast in the staff dining room when Clarice and her parents were scheduled to begin their journey home. I stepped away from my meal and into the hotel lobby just in time to see them getting into the limo through the revolving glass door. They all got into the back seat of the vehicle and disappeared behind its darkened windows. I waved, even though I knew that Clarice couldn't see me. When they were gone, I returned to my oatmeal and the usual chatter of the dining room.

We didn't learn until a few days later that there was a collision on 17 involving a limo en route to Stewart International. The limo had gotten sideswiped by a semi. Clarice, her parents, and the limo driver died at the scene. But the man in the trunk was still alive.

# CHAPTER 45

Lovato stopped a few hundred feet back from where he saw the Pinto turn into the woods. He began to move forward when he suddenly saw a black limo emerge from the trees and turn away from him. Lovato slowed down and kept a safe distance. He could almost make out the license plate number on the back of the vehicle. The plate itself was blue on gold.

"What the hell is going on in the woods?" he muttered to himself.

When the limo was out of sight, Lovato moved up to where the dirt road began and squinted into the forest. He wrestled with whether to make the turn or not and opted to just take careful note of where he was. He didn't want his cousin to end up in a shallow grave, but he had his family to think about. Rita promised to get in touch with him. How long should he wait?

Lovato knew that Rita had spoken to Ariti and that she had been picked up by the car he had seen on his block every day that Rita had worked at Hoffman's. It looked like Rita knew the driver. She didn't hesitate to get into the car. From a distance, it looked like they were talking. But the driver seemed to have an especially large head. It took a while for Lovato to realize it was a hat of some sort.

Ariti seemed to be a good sort when he'd met him at the hotel. He surrendered Rita's belongings only after ascertaining that Lovato was who he said he was and a respected business owner in the community. Even though the cops had eventually taken Rita's bag and had found heroin residue in it, Ariti had acted surprised and offered to help however he could. For a minute, Lovato wondered if Ariti, or someone else, had planted the heroin residue there. But who, and to what end? Rita had confessed to him that she had been trafficking drugs for a couple of weeks, but why would she be so careless?

Lovato contemplated going to the police, but Rita had made it clear that she didn't want to turn herself in. She thought she had a chance at getting away with this last caper, and he didn't want to deprive her of this opportunity. If he went to the police, he might keep her from getting killed. On the other hand, if Rita ended up in jail for the next ten years, she would never forgive him. Ariti had sent her a driver. The driver took her to this place in the woods.

Curiosity got the better of him. Lovato parked his car in a thicket and proceeded down the dirt path on foot. It was still fairly early in the day, but the woods always seemed dark and forbidding to him. He told himself he wouldn't walk for more than ten minutes. He lived in the country, but, at heart, he was a city boy. The sounds of the forest gave him the creeps. The deeper in he got, the louder the animal sounds became. Lovato was terrified of snakes and bears, and he knew that both lived in the Catskills. Still, he stumbled along in his Hush Puppies, trying to avoid roots.

Suddenly, he came to a clearing and quickly hid behind a maple. He saw a log house, the Pinto, and what appeared to be a small shed. He saw a woman leaning into the passenger window of the car with her arms on the sill. If he listened carefully, he could vaguely hear a feminine voice.

The door on the driver's side opened, and out came a tall man with a crazy-looking hat and sunglasses. The woman who had been leaning into the car backed up to allow Rita to get out. They all headed to the house, climbed the front steps, and entered. The woman seemed to scan the woods before closing the door behind her, and Lovato feared he had been spotted.

Lovato remained plastered to the trunk of the maple tree for a good ten minutes before stepping back onto the dirt road. He felt relieved to see a woman and a nice civilized-looking house in the woods instead of bunch of goons with machine guns and bad attitudes. But in the back of his mind, he still feared for his cousin's life.

And who was the cat in the hat?

154

# CHAPTER 46

The girls and I were completely horrified to hear the news about Clarice and her parents, and Susie was inconsolable.

"What did she do to deserve getting killed, aside from dating the wrong guy?" she cried. "I can't spend another minute in this place. My father is coming to pick me up this afternoon. The hell with Labor Day weekend."

Mary-Ann had her arm around her as they sat side-by-side on the double bed in our hotel suite. She had no soothing words for Susie; only her gentle touch. We all felt bereft.

Marsha said, "Maybe it was just an accident on the Interstate. It seems like those big trucks kill someone every other day. And it was raining a little that morning."

"Not everyone has a half-dead person in the trunk," I pointed out. "Who do you suppose that was?"

The local paper had not revealed the name of the person found in the trunk, but it did identify the individual as a male in critical condition from blunt-force trauma wounds to the head and torso.

"I'm going to take a wild guess that it was Denny," said Marsha. "I mean, we saw Clarice leave in a limo with her parents to go have dinner with Ariti. Then, probably the same limo came to pick them up to take them to the airport the next morning. Didn't Clarice say that Ariti organized their ride? When we spoke with Clarice, she was vague about where Denny was being held in custody. I think she had to sell her soul to Ariti and keep her mouth shut in exchange for – what? Money? Safety? Maybe Ariti didn't trust her."

We all looked at each other, and Mary-Ann said, "I certainly hope he didn't have Clarice killed because he was afraid she would tell us something that would expose him somehow. All she told us was that they had dinner at Ariti's house, Gina apologized, and they were brought back to the hotel at around 9 p.m. They were all looking forward to getting out of here. In fact, Clarice was ready to leave without saying good-bye to us. She said her father was in a big hurry."

We fell silent for a moment, as thoughts ricocheted around in our heads.

"I think we should speak with Ariti," I said.

"What are you, crazy?" asked Marsha.

"Why not?" I said. "One of our own gets killed right after socializing with our boss, and we aren't interested in what happened?"

"Of course, we're interested," said Mary-Ann. "We're just scared. People have been dying left and right around here, if you haven't noticed. I don't want to be the next casualty."

Susie sat sobbing into her Kleenex.

She said, "I won't be leaving here in a limo, that's for sure. My father's picking me up in our Buick Electra, and there'll be a revolver under the driver's seat. "

"Let's hope he doesn't have to use it," I said.

We all jumped at a knock at the door.

"Who is it?" we all screamed in unison.

"It's me," yelled Mark. "Are you all right?"

We could see the doorknob shaking, like he was on the verge of breaking in.

I quickly got up and went to the door.

"Mark?" I said, "Are you alone?"

"Of course, I'm alone," he said. "Who else would I be with?"

I opened the door and fell into his waiting arms.

"There's something fucked up going on around here," he said into my hair.

"That's an understatement," I said.

I took him by the hand and led him into the room.

"Did you hear the news?" asked Marsha.

"Yes, I did," said Mark. "I heard it, and I came straight here. It's on the news, you know. I saw it on a TV at the health club."

"What do you think we should do?" I asked him.

"I think you should keep way the hell out of it," he said. "All of you."

Susie said, "I'm leaving today."

156

"Not a bad idea," said Mark.

"Well," I said, "I'm sticking around until the bitter end."

I put my arm around Mark's waist, and continued, "I want to get to the bottom of all the crap that's been going on here all summer. If Clarice's death wasn't an accident, I don't want the perpetrator to get away with it."

Mary-Ann looked at me askew, and said, "For God's sake, Amy, there was a badly-injured man in the trunk of the vehicle she got killed in. We're dealing with some nasty people here. Why play investigative reporter now?"

"Let's just say that Clarice is speaking to me from the great beyond," I said.

"She's probably saying that she never knew what hit her," said Marsha.

"She knew more than what she told us," I said.

We chewed on that for a while, and then I said, "Just for the hell of it, I think I'll call Richard Lovato."

"Who's that?" asked Mark.

"Do you remember the waitress who disappeared, Rita?" I said. "Richard Lovato is her cousin. I wonder if he could help us connect the dots somehow."

"Do you have a number for him?" asked Mark.

"Yes," I said. "I'm the first one who took his number, when he came here to inquire about his cousin's disappearance. It seems like ages ago."

"Why would he want to talk to you?" asked Mark.

I looked around at the faces of my roommates, and said, "Why wouldn't he want to talk to me?"

I took out the napkin with Lovato's number written on it, and asked Mark to accompany me to the phone booth in the hotel lobby. I told the girls I would be back shortly and asked Susie not to leave before I had a chance to say good-bye to her.

When I got into the phone booth, it occurred to me that it was daytime and that Lovato was probably at his store. I had an operator connect us. When he answered, I said, "Is this Richard Lovato?"

He said, "Yeah?"

I identified myself, and he gave me a friendly hello. When I asked about
Rita, I could feel the silence grow heavy between us.

"Mr. Lovato?" I said.

"Yeah, I'm here," he said.

I asked him if he'd heard from Rita. He told me he couldn't talk to me from the store. I could tell he wanted to share something with me.

"Can you meet me somewhere in about a half-hour?" he asked.

Mark was watching me like a hawk outside the glass booth. He had his body between me and anyone who could read lips. I had a few hours before work, so I told Lovato I could meet him down at the Mountaintop.

Mark would be a couple of tables over, in case things got weird. But I suspected that Lovato was as concerned as I was about the strange happenings of that summer. Maybe he thought I had new information about his cousin. At the very least, I suspected we were on the verge of becoming partners in crime solving. All we had to do was not get killed in the process.

# CHAPTER 47

When Rita and Rocco entered the Ariti house, Gina told them her brother was out running an errand. Rocco had been in the house many times before and had a history with Gina. In fact, they had dated for years before Ariti broke them up. Ariti thought highly of Rocco. Rocco was a loyal and dependable employee. But Ariti feared that, in Rocco's line of work, he might not have much of a future.

Gina had been enraged with her brother for destroying their relationship, but finally comprehended that he was trying to protect her. She understood even more after she got her law degree and got involved in the family business. But that didn't keep her from continuing to have feelings for Rocco, even after she married Denny Martin.

It was hard for Gina to see Rocco with another woman, even after all these years. But Rita was an innocent party when it came to her love affair with Rocco, and Gina didn't hold it against her. Still, it bothered her. Gina had a jealous streak.

Rita had been married to that monster, Marty Gold, who Gina knew by reputation. Rita was lucky to escape with her life after she fled from him with a little bit of his money.

Rita was desperate. She saved herself by paying the bastard back and helped Ariti out with his business until Sabra returned to the United States to resume work after a close call with a hostile dealer. Rita wasn't above committing a criminal act, but did not possess a criminal heart. She was a woman who had spent most of her life down on her luck.

Her luck was about to change.

Gina sat them both down in the living room, on the same couch the O'Hares had occupied a few hours before. In anticipation of their arrival, she had placed a pot of hot coffee and a plate of biscotti on the coffee table, along with mugs, plates, teaspoons, sugar, and cream. Gina nestled back into one of the flowery chairs.

"We think it's best for the two of you to leave the country for a while," said Gina, looking into first Rocco's eyes, then Rita's. "You are both wanted by the police, and worse, and we don't want anything bad to happen to either one of you."

"Like Drew and Sabra?" asked Rocco.

"Yes," said Gina. "Just like Drew and Sabra."

"I think they were on their way to do one last exchange before they got popped," said Rocco.

Gina looked uncomfortable as she admitted, "Yes, there was going to be one last transaction, and then they were leaving the country. What happened to them was a mishap I am not proud of. You and Rita are done with the drug trade, and we're going to be a lot more careful about getting you out of here in one piece."

"Thanks for that," said Rita.

"Do you have a replacement for us?" asked Rocco, finally removing his hat.

Gina said, "We are all getting out of the drug business. It's dirty. George is high enough on the totem pole to pass it along to someone else. Maybe we'll get into the gambling racket, instead."

"Oh, great," said Rita. "Maybe you'll get to be a farmer now, honey."

Rocco gave her a side look and was about to say something when they all heard a scratching sound on the gravel driveway.

"Are you expecting anyone?" asked Rocco.

"Yes," said Gina. "That would be George with a surprise for you. How about we go meet him out back?"

The three of them rose and followed Gina through the kitchen to the back door. Ariti was emerging from a desert gold Chevy Camaro. Ariti stepped forward to embrace Rocco, and asked Rita, "May I?" before embracing her.

Ariti said, "It's good to see you alive and well. You were right to call me when you did, Rita."

"Thank you, Mr. Ariti."

He didn't tell her to call him George.

"This is what's going to happen," said Ariti. "You are going to stay here with us for the next few days. We're going to doctor up some records

160

for you and give you a wad of cash, including a large sum of Canadian dollars and English pounds. The car I just drove up in is yours, to get you to Toronto. You'll stay in Toronto for a few days, just like a pair of tourists. We have a couple of wedding bands for you, and you will be Mr. and Mrs. Michael and Gloria Turner from Dover, Delaware. You'll see that the car has Delaware plates. No wig for you, this time, Rita – or, I should say, 'Gloria.' The short hair is fine. Rocco, we're going to cut and color your hair before we take new pictures of you both."

Rita and Rocco remained silent.

"After your stay in Toronto, you will fly to Heathrow Airport in London and do a little more sightseeing."

"What happens to the car?" asked Rocco. "Does it remain in Toronto?"

"The car will remain at the Toronto Airport long-term parking facility until we figure out where to send you next. If things cool down here, you can fly back from London, pick up the car in Toronto, and await further instructions on where to go next. Understand?"

Rita and Rocco nodded in agreement. This was the out they were hoping for.

Ariti said, "Rita, I want you to know that most of the money for this trip is coming from the tips you took from the girls at Hoffman's. And the rest of it is coming from the tips that Sabra took before her untimely death. It's an unfortunate way to bankroll sudden escapes like this, but it's got to come from somewhere. You're not getting all of it. I've saved some to give the cocktail waitresses large bonuses after Labor Day weekend. They will get every bit of their hard-earned money back."

"I'm glad to hear that, Mr. Ariti. I really didn't feel right taking money from those girls. As an actual waitress, I know how hard they work for those tips."

Ariti went on, "For the next few days, I want you to keep out of sight. Take what you want from the kitchen. Mi casa es su casa. Be comfortable. Gina and I will be preparing you to leave. One of my guys is going to ditch the Pinto. Do you have anything in it that you need to remove?"

They both shook their heads.

161

"I didn't have any time to pack a bag," said Rita. "What am I supposed to do for clothes and stuff?"

"Gina will take your sizes and buy you all essentials tomorrow. For you, too, Rocco. After you leave here with your new IDs and money, you'll be on your own. Nobody will ever know you were here."

Nobody, except Richard Lovato. But Ariti didn't know that.

# CHAPTER 48

Mark brought me to the Mountaintop early. I sat at one booth, and Mark sat a couple of booths away where he could keep an eye on me but not eavesdrop on my conversation with Lovato. I told him that Lovato and I needed privacy. It was a time of day when business was slow. I hoped that Lovato would recognize me when he came in. I didn't want to leave my name at the hostess stand.

I saw him before he saw me. He was in jeans and a plaid shirt. He scanned the room before his eyes lit on me, and he came right over.

"Amy?" he said.

"Hi, Mr. Lovato," I said.

"Call me Richie," he said. "Mr. Lovato is my father."

It was an old joke, but it brought a smile to both of our faces. I told him to please sit down. A waiter was there almost instantly.

"What's good here?" asked Lovato.

"You can't go wrong with the roast pork on garlic bread," I said. "It's a house specialty."

"One of those," he said to the waiter. "With a Bud," he added.

"I'll have what he's having," I said.

After the waiter left, Lovato asked, "So, is it safe to talk here?"

"I sure hope so, Richie. A lot has gone on since the last time I saw you."

"Yeah, for me, too," he said.

"Do you want to go first, or should I?" I asked.

Lovato looked around nervously, and said, "Why don't you go first, Amy. I mean, you called me. You must have something to say."

I wondered if I could trust him. I had gotten paranoid in the last few weeks, but Lovato had never been a cause of concern to me. He was merely Rita's cousin, and I thought he was genuinely worried about her safety. I looked around the dining room before I began. There were a couple of families in there with loud children. I decided to just spill it.

"I don't know how much you know," I began, "but I think that Rita is out there running from the Mob."

"Yeah, that much I know," said Lovato.

"Do you know about the cocktail waitress and the security guard that got killed recently, and the other cocktail waitress that died with her parents in a limo accident on the way to Stewart International Airport?"

"Yeah, I heard about all that. I read the papers."

"Did you hear about the banged-up guy they found in the back of the limo?"

"Yeah. Do you know who he was? The papers didn't say."

"I have my theories," I said cryptically.

"Hey, if you know something, tell me," he said.

"All of these people worked for Hoffman's," I said. "The waitress and the security guard were a couple of drug runners who had worked together for years. The other waitress who got killed with her parents was a friend who got involved with the wrong man. She, her parents, and the limo driver may have actually died in an accident. But the guy in the trunk was no accident. I think that guy was my friend's former boyfriend, who made her pregnant and put her in the hospital."

"Nice guy," said Lovato. "What was he doing in the trunk?"

"I think he was placed there by people who were anxious to dispose of him – like his soon-to-be ex-wife, and maybe her brother."

"I'm following," said Lovato. "Is the brother anyone I know?"

"Yes, you know him," I said. "The brother is George Ariti, my boss over at Hoffman's. Rita's boss, too. In fact, everyone's boss except for the lousy boyfriend, and he may also have been working for Ariti somehow. He taught people how to play golf all day. Maybe he scored drugs for Ariti at night. Who knows?"

"I sure as hell don't. Nobody was more shocked than me when the cops came and found heroin in my cousin's bag."

"I can imagine," I said.

The waiter brought the food and beer, and we fell silent while he put everything on the table. He had more food and drink left on the tray, and I noticed that he brought it to Mark's table. I looked at Mark and he winked at me.

I didn't return his wink. Instead, I bit into my sandwich and gave Lovato a chance to bite into his."

"Very good," said Lovato with his mouth full. He swallowed and had a swig of the Bud before continuing.

"You know," he said, "this is the screwiest summer I ever saw. I'm a small businessman. I take care of my wife and kid and keep to myself. There have been Mob shakedowns in Monticello. Not so much in my town. Not yet, anyway. I left plenty of that kind of stuff behind in New Jersey. We moved to the country to avoid all that. Only, you can't avoid it. It seems to be everywhere."

"I'm from Long Island," I said. "It's everywhere there, too."

Lovato took another bite and looked at me while I spoke.

"I like Mr. Ariti very much," I said. "He's always treated me and the other girls with respect and fairness, but I think he might be in this up to his eyebrows."

Lovato swallowed and spoke while I chewed. Mark's eyes never left me. The kids started to chase each other around the dining room. Nobody but Mark and the waiter paid any attention to Lovato and me.

"Let me tell you about what I know," he said, "but you can't tell nobody."

My mouth was full, so I nodded in agreement.

"I'm not kidding, Amy. If I tell you this, you gotta keep it quiet. Otherwise, we'll be the ones in the cement shoes."

I nodded, and he went on.

"Rita came to me the other day. Her boyfriend got spooked when those two kids got shot up on 17, and he dumped her off at my house."

"I swallowed, and said, "Are we talking Rocco here?"

"Yeah, we're talking Rocco. She loves the guy. And he apparently loves her, too, because he dropped her off for her own safety, you know?"

I nodded.

"I told her I couldn't keep her around and that she should go to the police. But she has a record and was afraid she would be locked away for who-knows-how-long. And you can't trust the cops. Some of them protect the gangsters, you know?"

I didn't, but I wasn't surprised to hear it.

"Anyway," he continued, "Rita didn't know which way to turn, so she decided to call George Ariti. She said he owed her. For what, I don't know, and I was afraid to ask. I mean, I know she was trafficking drugs and all that. If she did anything else for him, I don't know about it."

I tried to imagine Ariti asking Rita for anything else, and I couldn't see it. I just shook my head and had a sip of Bud.

"So, I took Rita to a phone booth in Ellenville so she could place a call to him. He answered and told her he was sending a car. Rita told me to leave before her ride showed up, so I drove around the block and lay in wait, out of sight, you know?"

I told him to go on.

"So, a blue Pinto shows up, same car I seen before. It's the car that picked Rita up every time she went to Hoffman's. She gets in, and they take off. They don't know it, but I take off behind them."

I wiped my mouth on a napkin and looked at him.

"They drove for around fifteen minutes, and then the car turns into the woods, onto a dirt road. A minute later, a limo comes out and turns away from me. I don't know what to do, but, after a while, I get out of my car, and walk down the dirt road. I really messed up my shoes doing it, too. I don't like walking in the woods, but I needed to see where the driver brought Rita."

I asked Lovato, "Did you find out?"

"Yeah. He took her to a nice log house with a shed in the front yard. A woman came out to greet them. Seemed friendly enough, like she knew them."

"Did you say you saw a limo drive out?" I asked.

"Yeah, black limo with dark windows."

"Rocco brought Rita to Ariti's house," I said, "the same place Clarice and her parents went before they got killed."

Lovato stopped chewing and looked at me.

"Holy shit, Amy" he said, "pardon my language. Whadda we gonna do now?"

"That's what we've got to figure out, Richie."

# CHAPTER 49

Denny Martin died of his injuries in an ambulance en route to a hospital in Newburgh, New York. The limo that Denny was "riding" in when it crashed was registered in the name of a financial corporation in Lancaster, Pennsylvania. The limo driver had a standard New York State driver's license in the name Joseph McCardle. He was not a licensed chauffeur, but there was no requirement for him to be licensed as a chauffeur to drive the limo, so no laws had been broken. Further research revealed no criminal record for McCardle.

Denny's father was the founder and CEO of the company in Lancaster. Denny went to work for him early on as a broker, but Denny got himself arrested for shady dealings, lost his broker's license, and went to jail for a couple of years. His father wasn't above shady dealings himself. His company was a front for a big money laundering operation, but he was never found out. He wanted to keep it that way.

When Denny got out of prison, his father shipped him off to the New York Catskills where he could work in obscurity, put his criminal talents to good use, and contribute to the family corporation from a safe distance. He had a contact there: George Ariti. Ariti was Denny's age, but far more accomplished and polished enough to fly under the radar. Ariti was well regarded in his community. He knew how to balance give and take. And he had a mutually beneficial relationship with local law enforcement.

As a kid growing up in a wealthy family, Denny was sent to the best schools, got his MBA, and learned how to golf really well. When Denny made it to Hoffman's, Ariti put him to work as a golf pro under his legal name, and had him handle the financial end of various jobs under an assumed name. Ariti didn't have Denny do anything that would put him in the line of fire. Illicit associates never saw Denny face-to-face, nor did they know his real name. Denny spoke to people on an untraceable phone line and transacted business with a high level of integrity. He was solely accountable to Ariti, who became his friend and mentor.

At some point, Ariti introduced Denny to his kid sister, Gina, who had recently earned a law degree from Columbia. Gina was also not going to get her hands dirty. Ariti required Gina's legal mind and Denny's financial mind, but, otherwise, he wanted to keep both out of harm's way.

Gina and Denny eventually married and had children, but Gina had a thriving criminal law practice in White Plains, New York, and Denny spent most of the year at Hoffman's as a golf pro so he could have something legitimate to report to the IRS. This worked out for them for years, as long as Gina turned a blind eye to Denny's philandering, and Denny remained blissfully unaware of Gina's trysts with her old love, Rocco. Ariti knew about both but stayed out of their relationship. It was enough that he broke up Gina's adolescent love affair with Rocco, fearing that Rocco's days were numbered. It was Ariti who had placed Rocco in his dangerous position to begin with. It was Rocco who physically met with the drug lords and negotiated with the heads of warring families.

Like Ariti, Rocco wasn't an evil man by nature. He had a sense of honor and genuine compassion. He would have made a poor hit man. His biggest weakness was that he was addicted to gambling. Sometimes, he got in over his head, and he had to do whatever he could to stay alive. Ariti wasn't a gambler, but, sometimes, he also got in over his head. It was an easy thing to do in his field.

When Rocco met Rita for the first time, he had been sent by Marty Gold to go after his wife and throw her in the Hudson. Not having the stomach to kill anyone, and having debts of his own, Rocco talked Marty into a deal that would benefit all of them and leave no dead bodies to rise to the surface.

Unbeknownst to Marty Gold, Rocco was also closely aligned with George Ariti. Ariti had gotten into debt with the drug lords in Sullivan County when his top two traffickers, Drew and Sabra, had to leave the country for their own protection. Rocco saw a way to fix his problem, too; all without getting Rita killed.

As time went by, it became particularly important to Rocco that Rita be protected because he had fallen in love with her, and now had fantasies of becoming a farmer in Kansas and raising children and corn.

At this point, everybody had been paid off. Rita and Rocco were in Ariti's safe house until they embarked on their own journey with carefully falsified papers and clothing provided by Rocco's ex, Gina. They had no idea that Denny had been pummeled with a nine iron by Gina in Ariti's shed the night before, before taking one last trip the next morning in the limo provided by Denny's father in Lancaster. After a crash had killed all passengers but Denny, Denny died before he could say anything to the authorities about how he had gotten into the trunk. And what would he have been able to say? The man who had been hired to kill him was dead, and the other deceased passengers were the ones who had put Denny in jail for aggravated assault with intent to commit great bodily harm. They wouldn't have been sorry to see him go.

The long-haul truck driver who swerved into the limo survived without a scratch. He tearfully confessed that he had momentarily fallen asleep behind the wheel.

The crashed limo would be linked to Denny's father in Pennsylvania. The father would say that he had gifted the vehicle to his son years before to help him start a transportation business when he was released from prison. The name on the registration had never been changed, and, for that, Denny's father was charged a one hundred dollar fine. Mr. Martin arranged for Denny to be buried in the family plot in Lancaster. Gina attended the small funeral with her children and Ariti. Nobody in the family knew that Gina and Denny were on the verge of divorce, so Gina stopped the divorce proceedings and received a substantial inheritance from her deceased husband's estate.

Nobody, outside of Ariti and Gina, knew that Denny's death ride began at Ariti's house in the woods. Nobody but Richard Lovato and Amy.

And nobody but Gina knew that she had organized the crash.

# CHAPTER 50

Susie was gone by the time I got back to my room, and Marsha was the only one there.

"What the hell took you so long?" asked Marsha. "Susie's father picked her up an hour ago."

"Damn it," I said, "I lost track of the time."

"You've been on the phone with Rita's cousin all this time?"

"No. He had me meet him at the Mountaintop, and we ended up schmoozing longer than expected."

"Did you learn anything?"

"Nothing new, unfortunately."

From the look she gave me, I couldn't tell if Marsha believed me or not. But she said, "Well, I have something new for you."

My interest peaked.

"Yeah? Tell me."

"Ariti himself stopped over before they left. He introduced himself to Susie's father, and said he was sorry to see Susie go before the end of the summer. He also said that he understood why."

"Sounds decent enough," I said.

"He then gave Susie a very fat envelope," Marsha said.

"Probably her final pay," I said.

"And then some," said Marsha.

"Meaning?"

"There was a lot more than her final pay in there. Ariti asked her to open the envelope, right in front of all of us. Susie's eyes nearly popped out. The paycheck was miniscule, of course, but the cash in there was huge."

"Define 'huge,'" I said.

"Thousands of dollars huge, I'm guessing," said Marsha.

"Did Ariti have anything to say about it?" I asked.

"Yes," said Marsha. "He said he knew our tips went missing several times during the summer, and this was his way of making up for it."

"I wonder if we'll all get an envelope like that?" I said.

"He told us we would," Marsha said. "We may even get more for sticking around through the end of the holiday.

"There are only three of us left," I said. "Labor Day weekend is going to be a bear. And, with the season almost over, Ariti isn't going to be able to find anyone else to pinch hit."

"Unless Rita is waiting in the wings," joked Marsha.

I laughed, and said, "Wouldn't that be something? I wonder if she'll be wearing a wig."

"Don't worry about it," said Marsha. "Ariti will tag one or two of the regular waitresses to help out. They can manage the slower stations, if there is such a thing on that holiday."

As I picked up my robe and walked toward the bathroom, I asked, "Where's Mary-Ann?"

Marsha said, "She was pretty blue after Susie left, so she went down to the lake to meet up with Louis and some of his friends."

"That'll distract her," I said. "Still, I hope she breaks up with that jerk before she leaves in a couple of weeks. I never liked that guy."

"They did make it through a whole summer together," said Marsha. "They've got to have something good going on."

"I suppose," I said.

Mary-Ann showed up just as I was collecting my robe and flipflops. I gave her a quick hug, and said, "I'm sorry I wasn't here when Susie left. Are you okay?"

"I'm all right," she said, "but it's sad to keep losing people I'm close to. First Clarice, and now Susie."

"Not Rita?" I asked.

"I never really got to know Rita," she said. "So, no, I don't miss Rita. Did you find out anything about her from her cousin?"

"Afraid not," I said. "She and Rocco are like gone with the wind."

"Better than whacked," muttered Marsha.

"Oh," said Mary-Ann, "I saw Ariti's sister down at the lake. I think she was there alone. At least, I didn't see any kids with her. She was working on her tan, although with her dark olive skin, it seemed like overkill."

"You can't be too tan," I said, noticing that my own olive skin against my white robe had darkened quite a bit that summer.

"Did she say anything to you?" asked Marsha.

"Actually, I went over to say hello to her," said Mary-Ann.

"What did you do that for?" asked Marsha.

"No harm in being friendly," said Mary-Ann. "We just exchanged a few niceties. She didn't remember me from our brief introduction at the club, to tell you the truth. But she did ask about you, Amy."

"Really?" I said, intrigued. "What did she want to know?"

We both sat down on the edge of one of the beds, and Marsha sat on the edge of another. The room suddenly felt too big and too crammed full of furnishings.

"She asked if you were still around, and I told her you were," said Mary-Ann. "She said that she had met you at the lake earlier in the summer and had enjoyed talking with you."

Mary-Ann thought for a moment, and added, "She said she would catch you later in the lounge or nightclub."

"I shouldn't be too hard to catch," I said. "I'll be wearing stilettos and holding a twenty-pound tray over my head with one hand. How fast can I run?"

—

I was just signing out for the night when Gina came up to me, seemingly out of nowhere. It wasn't that busy of a night, and Ariti told me and the girls that we could leave early. The bartenders could handle any additional orders themselves.

"Hi, Amy," she said. "Remember me?"

"Of course, I do. Gina, right? How are you?"

Gina was dressed in casual clothing, like she had gone to bed and set an alarm to meet me at quitting time. It was nearly 3 a.m.

"I'm great," she said.

She didn't look that great to me. She looked like she would have been better off sleeping through the alarm. Her dark hair was disheveled, and her only makeup was a smear of mauve lipstick.

"What brings you here at this hour?" I asked. "Are you alone?"

"Yes," she said.

Gina was sleepy and agitated at the same time. I could sense her struggle to keep her voice calm.

I asked, "Is everything all right? Is there anything I can do for you?"

Gina said, "Can I trust you, Amy?"

I looked at her in surprise, and said, "I'm pretty trustworthy, but you're making me nervous, Gina. Why would you get up in the middle of the night to tell me a secret?"

What did she want from me? I was just a college girl working my way through school. I'd be gone soon. I hoped that Mark would emerge from the nightclub any minute and walk me out of there.

I asked, "Can this wait until tomorrow, Gina? I just worked for the past ten hours, and I would really like to get some sleep."

"No Mountaintop tonight?" she asked.

"No, not tonight," I said. "I'll be with my boyfriend tonight. Summer's almost over, and you know how that is. People get frantic to wrap things up and move things forward."

"Yes, I am frantic to do that, myself, Amy. And I'm leaving tomorrow morning."

"So, why come to me?"

"Because I think you know things, and I need to know that you will keep your mouth shut."

Gina sounded a little less sleepy and a lot testier.

"I don't know what you think I know, but I can assure you that I am no threat to you."

"Never let me believe that you're a threat to me, Amy," said Gina.

"I think you may be threatening *me*, Gina."

"You better believe it."

She left me standing there feeling like I should take my money and run, maybe that night with Mark in the Carmen Ghia. Maybe we could hide out with Mark's parents in Flatbush.

173

That's what I was thinking when Mark walked up, and said, "Ready to go, babe?"

All I could say was, "You better believe it."

# CHAPTER 51

Rita and Rocco sat in the Camaro in the middle of the Peace Bridge that connects Buffalo, New York, to Ft. Erie, Ontario. They had their doctored passports handy, in preparation for going through U.S. Customs and Border Protection.

"How you doing, Gloria?" Rocco teased, as Rita fussed with her short brown hair and adjusted her glasses.

"I'll be fine once we get through Border Patrol, Michael," she said. "Nice to get out of Dover and away from all those Turners. I can't wait to see the Royal Ontario Museum and that new CN Tower that's being built. Wow!"

"You've been doing your homework," said Rocco. "Good for you." Rocco smiled at Rita, and squeezed her hand.

"Not too much longer now, but I can't believe all this damn traffic," he said. "We're really locked in here."

"Well, it's summer and Niagara Falls is a big attraction," said Rita. "Look, we can see the falls from this bridge. That little boat down there is called Maid of the Mist."

"You know what?" said Rocco, "There's is no big rush to get to Toronto. We're supposed to be on vacation, right? If we ever get off this damn bridge, why don't we spend a little time seeing the sights. We can even take a ride on that little boat. Whaddya say?"

Rita looked at Rocco with his newly cut black hair and pale eyes and fell a little more in love with him.

"Maybe we can pretend we're on our honeymoon," she said.

"Hey, this is Niagara Falls," he said. "We can probably get married for real in about two minutes."

Rita smiled at him, and said, "But we're already married, Mr. Turner."

"Oh, yeah," Rocco said.

"Don't forget it," said Rita. "We're getting closer to Border Patrol."

"Yeah, one inch at a time," said Rocco. "But we're just like everyone else now. Just inching along to go through Customs like regular folks. And the only baggage we got contains socks and underwear, nothing illegal. I feel free, Rita. For the first time in decades, I feel like I'm on a straight path, and I'm digging it. And I'm really digging it with you."

Rita allowed herself a moment of pure joy. If they managed to get out of the U.S. in one piece, she didn't see any reason to return. Lots of young draft dodgers were immigrating to Canada. Why not a nice, industrious couple in their middle thirties looking to start a new life in a new country? Not one that was constantly at war.

They finally made it to Customs. The agent asked a few questions about what they were doing in Canada, how long they were planning to be there, and where they were going. He flipped open their passports and noted they didn't get around much.

"We're newlyweds," said Rocco, with exuberance. "We're on our honeymoon."

"Well, congratulations," said the agent looking, first, at their faces, and then at their passport photos, and back again. Satisfied, he stamped both booklets and told them to enjoy their stay.

Rita cringed when she heard Rocco say, "Thanks, officer," but the agent just waved them through, and they were on their way.

"Sorry, I slipped up," said Rocco.

"No harm done," said Rita. "We've made it into Canada. Can you believe it?"

"Yeah, but we're not out of the woods yet."

"What do you mean?"

"You met Gina, right?"

"Ariti's sister? Yes. What about her?"

"You know I used to see her, right?"

"How would I know? This is the first I've heard of it."

"It was years ago, but George broke us up. He thought his little sister would be safer with that pig, Denny. But Gina and I continued to see each other on the sly. We were discreet and all, but I think that Denny knew. He didn't say anything because he had plenty of women on the side. Gina could live with the floozies – they meant nothing – but she couldn't

176

handle women of any quality that she saw as competition. It's not that she loved Denny. She just didn't want to be outdone."

Rita visibly deflated at his confession.

"Are you still involved with Gina, Rocco?"

"No! Hell, no. When you came into the picture, my whole deal with Gina went out the window. I mean, I really love you, Rita. There's nobody else but you. I swear."

"She was being so nice," said Rita. "Does she know we're involved?"

"Sure, she knows. That's what worries me a little."

"But she went shopping for us, for Christ's sake. Do you even know what's in your suitcase?"

"Sure, I do. I looked through it this morning before we left. I wanted to make sure there was a razor in there. Nothing exploded."

"You know, I wouldn't have gotten implicated in anything until someone found heroin residue in the bag I carried back and forth to Hoffman's. Could Gina have planted the heroin there?"

Rocco thought for a moment, and said, "It's possible."

"My God, Rocco, could she have planted more residue in this car? It's a miracle they didn't search the vehicle at Border Patrol. If there's heroin in this car and we're discovered with it, we can go away for years."

Rocco said, "Let's skip on the boat ride, for now. We're going to drive into the country somewhere and inspect this vehicle and both of our suitcases. Just hang tight and try not to panic."

To ease their anxiety, the couple traveled in silence until Rocco pulled onto a deserted road in Kingsville, Ontario, near Lake Erie. It was not the first time he had inspected a vehicle. He asked Rita to get out of the car. It was hot and muggy. Rita sat under a walnut tree on top of a raincoat provided by Gina early that morning. She swatted at gnats while Rocco painstakingly searched the Camaro. He even slid under the car to see if there was anything hidden beneath the chassis. Rita was impressed with his attention to minute detail.

Rocco checked both suitcases and found nothing. There were no false bottoms. There was a blanket in the trunk, along with towels, umbrellas, and other beach paraphernalia. Rocco carefully lifted each item and found three well-sealed plastic bags of heroin under the blanket.

177

"Son of a bitch," he hissed. "She tried to frame us."

Rocco slammed down the trunk and backed away from the car, clutching his arms and breathing hard. He walked in circles to try to calm himself.

Rita got up from the ground and went to him.

"This is insane, Rocco. Ariti sent us here to get us out of harm's way, not put us in more danger."

"This isn't George's doing," he said. "Gina's behind this. She's always looking to settle a score. She puts George at risk with this kind of stunt, too. She belongs in a nuthouse."

"Well, for Christ's sake, what are we supposed to do now?" asked Rita.

"The first thing we're going to do is ditch these bags of heroin," said Rocco. "Jeez, there must be a hundred-thousand-dollars-worth of smack in here."

Rita said, "You're not thinking of selling it, are you?"

"No," said Rocco. "I said I'm done with all that."

"Well, you can't throw those plastic bags into the lake. They'd probably float. How about burying them?"

"The soil is too shallow and rocky here," said Rocco, prodding the ground with the toe of his shoe. "Wait, I have an idea."

Rocco got into the car and came out with an emptied-out bag from MacDonald's. He squatted on the ground and filled the bag a quarter of the way with dirt and gravel. Rita watched from a distance while he went back to the trunk and carefully removed each sack of heroin, one at a time, and emptied them into the MacDonald's bag. He then rolled the top of the bag down and shook it so that the heroin combined with the earth. He was careful to not spill a drop.

"What in the world are you doing?" asked Rita.

"I'm going to scatter dear old dad in Lake Erie," said Rocco.

"I'm very sorry for your loss," said Rita. "I'm guessing that we won't be going to Toronto or London."

"Nope, neither of those. Who knows who would show up at our door?"

"You know that after you ditch dear old dad, you're going to have to also get rid of your clothes and wash your hands very thoroughly. And you're going to have to do all that before you get back into the car."

Rocco said, "I'm looking at that lake right now. I'm going to walk right over there and send dad downstream, after which I'm gonna take a little swim and rinse out those baggies. I've got a week's worth of clothing in that suitcase. There's even an extra pair of shoes. I'll dry off with one of the beach towels in the trunk and change in the car. Then, we'll ditch the wet stuff in some office park dumpster."

"Sounds like a plan," said Rita, "but what about the car?"

"What about the car?" asked Rocco.

"Don't we have to get rid of the car, too?"

"Hey, after we get rid of the heroin and make sure there's not a trace left, then the car is clean, and we have no worries."

"But what if the car isn't clean? Maybe it's used for trafficking dope into Canada and Mexico? Maybe we've just been used as unwitting mules," said Rita. "Maybe we get approached by people who are expecting their packages, and we don't have them anymore. Did Gina just set us up to get killed?"

"Mrs. Turner, we're not going to stick around Canada long enough to find out."

179

# CHAPTER 52

Earlier in the summer, Ariti had taken me into his confidence and asked me to keep an eye on Sabra and Drew. He acted like he only *suspected* them of drug trafficking, but he clearly had hired them for that purpose, and not for the first time. Why try to turn me into a confederate? Why the smokescreen? He was clearly involved, unless he was trying to protect someone. Like his sister.

Gina had clearly gotten up in the middle of the night, looking scruffy and deranged, to threaten me for no good reason. What did she think I had on her? Clarice had told me that Gina had apologized to her about the attack on the path, which she had attributed to her husband, Denny. What else did she think I knew?

Mark and I discussed my 3 a.m. encounter with Gina, even though I was warned to keep my mouth shut. He told me he thought I should go to Ariti.

"Are you trying to get me killed?" I asked.

Mark gave me a get-real look, and said, "I've been working here longer than you. I know that Ariti has always taken care of his little sister. She's very smart, but she's also out of her mind. From what I understand, she did go to Columbia, but she never passed the bar exam. When she's here, she's hardly ever out of Ariti's sight, unless she's down at the lake. Ariti pays the lifeguards extra to keep an eye on her when she's there."

"Where'd you hear all this?" I asked.

"Denny got drunk and spouted off at the Mountaintop one night. I was within earshot. Plus, I'm friends with the lifeguards."

"I don't understand," I said. "I thought that Gina had a successful law practice in Westchester County."

"That's a bunch of crap," said Mark. "If she has any law practice at all, she's advising her own brother. I think Ariti paid Denny off to marry his sister. Did you ever wonder why Denny mostly spent his time here, without her?"

"I never gave it much thought," I said. "I just figured it was a part of their lifestyle."

"Go to Ariti," Mark said, again. "He apparently trusts you."

"You want me to tattle on his potentially-murderous sister?" I asked.

"I want you to report that she threatened you, yes. I want you to finish out the summer and be with me as long as possible. I'm being a little selfish. I want you here, and I want you safe."

"Come with me," I said.

"You go by yourself," said Mark. "I won't be far off."

—

The next afternoon, I told Marsha and Mary-Ann I had a call to make and slipped out the door. I was already in uniform for work.

I made a beeline for Ariti's office, and hoped he'd be there. I wasn't at all sure that Mark had given me the best advice, but, if Gina had been honest with me the day before, she was already off the premises.

I knocked gently on the door and took a fortifying breath. Ariti asked, "Who is it?"

"It's Amy, Mr. Ariti. May I come in?"

I waited a minute, and Ariti answered the door, much like the other time I had been to his office.

"Is everything okay, Amy?" he asked, with his brow furrowed.

"There's something I need to talk to you about."

"Come in, my dear," he said.

I followed him, and he gestured toward a chair. The office was dark as hell. I felt like I was entering a tomb. Ariti was in his usual black suit. Once I was seated, he leaned a haunch against the edge of his meticulously neat desk and waited for me to speak.

I began, "Sometime back, you asked me to keep an eye on Sabra and Drew, and they ended up getting killed. As you suspected, they were involved in drug trafficking, but their execution still shook me."

Ariti said, "What makes you think they were executed?"

"According to the news, they were both shot in the head on the way to a drug deal. That doesn't sound like an accident to me."

"No, it doesn't," said Ariti. "They got in with the wrong people. Sad, but true."

I looked him in the eyes, and asked, "Did you have anything to do with their murder, Mr. Ariti?"

I saw his jaw work as he contemplated how to respond.

"I did not," he said.

I continued, "My friend Clarice and her parents recently died in a car crash after having dinner with you and your sister. Do you know how that could have happened? I mean, do you think it was just an accident?"

Ariti's eyes hardened, and he asked, "Are you accusing me of setting up a hit on Clarice and her parents? I had nothing to do with that either."

I shifted in my seat, sensing danger.

"I'm not accusing you of anything, Mr. Ariti. You've been nothing but good to me. But I've had recent dealings with your sister that *do* have me worried."

Ariti rubbed his eyes, and asked, "What has Gina done now?"

"She threatened me, Mr. Ariti. She came to me at 3 a.m., accusing me of knowing things and warning me to keep my mouth shut. I didn't know what she was talking about, but she seemed unhinged. It scared me. I don't want to leave you shorthanded, but I need to know if I should go home right now. I don't want to be the next casualty around here. I love this place, and I would like to return next year, as we discussed, but not if I'm at risk."

Ariti shook his head slowly, and said, "May I confide in you, Amy?"

He had asked me that question before. God knew what I was about to hear, but I said, "I came here to have a confidential conversation with you, so, yes, you can."

Ariti got up and sat down in the chair behind his desk. He looked at me over his nested hands, and said, "My sister is a paranoid schizophrenic. It began when she was about eighteen. Medications got her through most of her schooling, but her delusions increased as she got older. She became violent. One time, she set up a hit on her boyfriend because she thought he was cheating on her. Fortunately, I was able to call it off before anything happened. I sent the boyfriend packing before any harm could come to him and introduced her to Denny, who was working for me at the time. I thought if she had a husband and children, her condition would improve. But it did not."

"Gina has hurt many people over the years, some fatally," continued Ariti. "I have always covered for her, and the local police have looked the other way because of my standing in the community. But, this summer, Gina went completely haywire. People were going down left and right. She was even behind Denny's death. That didn't surprise me. But innocent people, like Clarice and her parents and my driver, also died, thanks to Gina. And now it sounds like she's coming after you. I can't have that, Amy."

"What are you going to do, Mr. Ariti?"

"I'm going to have her committed to a mental health facility where she can get the help she needs. There's a good one in White Plains. I've already checked into it. All I have to do is place a call, and they'll pick her up."

"What about her children?"

"They have a nanny they're fond of. She will take care of them for now."

"So, am I safe if I stay?"

"You're safe," said Ariti. "You have my word."

I don't know why, but I believed him.

# CHAPTER 53

Fearing for their lives, Rocco and Rita considered turning themselves in to the U.S. Marshalls to see if they qualified for the United States Federal Witness Protection Program, but Rocco had a problem with turning on Ariti. There was too much good blood between them. For them, it wasn't all business.

"George sent us to Canada for our own protection," said Rocco. "It was Gina who turned on us. I just know it. It wouldn't be for the first time with me."

"So," said Rita, "what do we do?"

"We place a call to George, and he tells us our next move. He needs to know that we're no longer in the drug business and that we just want to live our life in peace. We've paid our dues."

"I thought it was impossible to get out of the Mob," said Rita.

"Not if you have friends in high places," said Rocco.

Rocco found a phone booth and placed a call to Ariti's private line. Ariti answered and immediately asked if they were all right. Rocco told him what he had found in the Camaro.

"I hope you got rid of it," said Ariti.

"Nobody will ever find it, and I thoroughly cleaned the car," said Rocco.

"You cleaned it, you own it," said Ariti. "Consider it a wedding present, wherever you end up. The car is registered in the name Michael Turner. Is that who you're going to be now?"

"For the time being. But you can still call me Rocco."

There was a brief lull before Ariti said, "I put Gina away. She got into too much trouble this summer, and the losses were too high."

"Is she back in the place in White Plains?" asked Rocco.

"She is. Maybe for good, this time. But you and Rita disappear into whatever life you choose. Wherever you end up, don't let me know."

# CHAPTER 54

Labor Day weekend came and went. Marsha, Mary-Ann, and I really raked it in. Our summer at Hoffman's was ending, and we wondered if we would ever see each other again.

Mary-Ann was remaining in the Catskills with Louis. Marsha and I still didn't like him, but he made her happy, so we accepted her decision with grace. She had her college transcripts transferred to Sullivan County Community College. If she was still with Louis the following summer, she'd likely return to Hoffman's. But she wouldn't be living in the cabin with us.

Marsha and Max broke up, but she was okay with it. She was heading back to the University of Richmond, where she was a political science major. I hoped that we would keep in touch because we had gotten quite close that summer.

Mark and I would continue to see each other for a while, but I was returning to college in Boston, and he was going to graduate school in Cleveland, so our paths were not likely to cross much during the school year. He loved me and I loved him, and what a great way to leave things.

Ariti gave Mary-Ann, Marsha, and me the same wad of cash that Susie got, except a little bigger.

Before my father came to pick me up, I got a surprise visit from Richard Lovato. He told me he had heard from Rita and that she and Rocco were doing well.

"Did she tell you where they are?" I asked.

"She wouldn't tell me," he said, "but they're on a farm somewhere. Do you think they're hippies now? Peace and love and dancing around with flowers in their hair?"

It was the least likely scenario for Rita and Rocco, but I said, "I sure hope so, Richie."

I couldn't imagine a happier ending.

# CHAPTER 55

I never did make it back to Hoffman's the following summer. I knew that I could never relive the excitement of 1973, and, in truth, the Catskills had already gone past their heyday. Ironically, I ended up cocktail waitressing at a resort in Lancaster, Pennsylvania, where Denny Martin was from. The Amish Country was a far cry from the Borscht Belt, but the uniforms were equally slutty.

There was no shared cabin in Lancaster. I lived in a boarding house run by an elderly Mennonite lady. She shook her head mournfully every time she saw me leave for work in my hot pants and thigh-high boots. She liked me, though, because I chatted with her amiably and never brought a man back to my room. She knew I was just working my way through college.

I did have a boyfriend there. He had been a professional tennis player and managed the tennis facility at the resort. He improved my game, but, in the end, he was too old for me, and there were signs that he had a parallel life outside of our relationship. I didn't want to fall into the same trap that Clarice had fallen into.

I had few friends in Lancaster. The one other person who lived in the boarding house was a strange young man who never spoke. However, every time KC & Sunshine Band sang, "That's the Way (I Like It)" on the radio, he became a mattress-jumping, finger-clicking dancing fool. Otherwise, I never heard a sound out of him. Without living with the other waitresses, there was little intimacy between us. It was more private, but a lot lonelier. I left before the summer was out and went to work as a typist at my college. Too bad I couldn't type.

I missed the people and experiences I had come to know at Hoffman's – all of my roommates, George Ariti and Richard Lovato, Leo and his sauerkraut juice, all the performers I had met back stage, the Mountaintop, and the lake. I missed the gravel path and the cabin it led to, with its wall-to-wall beds filled with the voices and laughter of young college girls having an adventure. I even missed Rita, with her wig and secrets. I was happy to learn that a fulfilling life was still possible for her and her Rocco.

I kept in touch with a few people for a while, but as the years went by, we all got caught up in our own lives. I went on to get my PhD in Psychology at the University of Chicago. One day, I ran into Mark at a conference in Cincinnati, Ohio. He had gotten his doctorate in Criminology. We discovered that we had professional interests in common, along with reignited love interests, so I ended up marrying the boy from Flatbush, after all. We both became special agents for the FBI, and live in Washington, D.C. Sometimes, we take on private investigation jobs.

And we named our baby daughter Clarice.

# Acknowledgments

Many thanks to Amy Izatt and Dorothy Deaton for their friendship and excellent editing support. Much love and appreciation to my husband, Grant Holland, a great editor and patient, painstaking production coordinator. And a big thank you to all the amazing people that I met in my youth in the Catskills. You filled my life with richness in those best of times.

# About the Author

Mindy Littman Holland spent the summers of her youth in the hotels and bungalow colonies of New York's Catskill Mountains. When she was a teenager in the early 1970s, she worked as a cocktail waitress at a popular resort to help pay her way through college. She met an older woman on the job who had lots of secrets and who mysteriously disappeared. For nearly fifty years, Mindy thought about what might have happened to her. Mindy's rumination led her to write *Catskill Murder Mystery*.

Mindy is also the author of *Wait Until You're Fifty: A Woman's Journey Into Midlife*; *The Rebirth of Gershon Polokov*; *All My Funny Ones: A Collection of Short Stories*; and *Days of Wine and COVID: Fifty-Seven Stories of Pandemic Proportions*.

She lives with her husband, Grant, in Santa Fe, New Mexico. Visit her website at mindylittmanholland.com.